BORN TO BE STYLED

SPELLBOUND HOUND MAGIC AND MYSTERY BOOK 6

JEANNIE WYCHERLEY

Born to be Styled
Spellbound Hound Magic and Mystery Book 6

BY
JEANNIE WYCHERLEY

Sign up for Jeannie's newsletter:
www.subscribepage.com/JeannieWycherleyWonky

Born to be Styled was edited by Christine L Baker

Cover design by Cover Affairs
Formatting by Tammy
Proofreading by Johnny Bon Bon

Please note: This book is set in England in the United Kingdom.
It uses British English spellings and idioms.

Born to be Styled is gratefully dedicated to my own awesome dog groomers.

Firstly, Yvonne in Chaddesden
and
secondly, Ali in Talaton.

And to all dog groomers, everywhere!

CHAPTER ONE

Toby was minding his own business.

On this occasion, minding his own business took the form of improving his wizarding knowledge. Mrs Crouch, his next-door neighbour, had recently bought him a book from the Dogs Trust charity store downtown in Sun Valley, jammed full of all kinds of interesting information about British wildlife. Being the kind of dog he was, a schnauzer-collie-whippet-terrier-thingie of the most magickal and spellbound kind, his love for the outdoors knew no bounds and he wanted to learn as much as caninely possible about every element of it. Most of the wildlife identified in the book—*which had photos and diagrams and an index and everything!*—could only be found in the countryside, so Toby had taken himself off for a walk in the nearby wood at the end of the road behind the house behind his house. If you see what I mean.

Phew!

Toby's mind was a complicated place. Spellbound as a puppy by his beloved original owner, Old Joe, he could talk to witches and wizards and other magickal folk *and* be understood by them. He'd also been gifted a great capacity for learning and retaining knowledge. One of his greatest desires in life—besides having a pantry full of sammich fillings—was to become a glorious wizard.

To that end, having been reading up about voles in his magnificent wildlife book the previous evening while Clarissa Page, Old Joe's granddaughter and Toby's new hooman, tippity-tapped away on her laptop writing newspaper articles for *The Celestine Times*, Toby had risen with the dawn this morning to go in search of vole habitats. He'd proven himself to be not much of a vole hunter—not that he'd ever hunt and kill anything or anyone, with the possible exception of The Pointy Woman—but he'd had tremendous fun looking. In addition, he'd enjoyed several pleasant early morning chats, one with a fox and one with a pheasant. He very much hoped that neither of them would bump into the other after he'd left.

Chomp, chomp.

Feeling peckish, he'd skipped home just as the neighbourhood began to wake up. Men and women in suits, with slightly damp hair and smelling fresh from showers, sprang out of their houses and hurried to their cars. The old lady five doors down swept her step and the path to her house as she did every morning and had probably done for the past sixty-odd years. The toaster at the house next to hers had set off their smoke alarm, which seemed to be an occupational hazard whenever they used it. And that was often. Across the road, kids screamed, parents yelled back at them, cats slunk out of their houses seeking some peace and quiet, and a supermarket delivery van blocked the end of the road, causing mayhem for the commuters.

Toby barked a good morning to the lady with the broom and another to Moriarty, the black cat who lived directly across the road, but he didn't stop to chat. Not today. He was in too much of a rush. There was breakfast to be eaten and Clarissa to be hugged, and then he could settle down in his wizard shack and read another couple of sections of his book!

Pawesome!

He burst through his dog flap and into the

kitchen, startling Clarissa who was taking an egg out of the fridge. She jumped so high the egg flew out of her hand.

Toby had a split second to react. He could levitate the egg and return it to safety ... or he could let it drop.

He chose the latter.

The egg hit the tiled floor with a pleasantly sharp *crrrick*, spilling its contents at Clarissa's feet.

"Urgh!" Clarissa jumped back to escape egg white staining her black leggings. Too late. "Look what you made me do," she griped. "I think you need a bell outside the door to let me know you're about to burst in!"

"Soz," said Toby. "Would you like me to clean it up for you?" He didn't wait for her to respond, just began licking up the raw egg. *Ooh, the yolk is delicious!* He didn't care so much for the eggshell, however. No wonder hoomans tended not to eat those.

"I suppose you'll be wanting some breakfast?" Clarissa asked. "What would you like today? We have ..." She leaned over to open the cupboard door next to the sink where she kept his food. "So, we have chicken and rice, tuna and pasta, beef and vegetable ... or rabbit."

None of these were actually as exciting as they sounded. They were tins of carefully formulated dog food with all the correct nutrients and nothing in the way of pizzazz. Toby would quite happily have finished off a plate of *actual* tuna and pasta, but that wasn't genuinely on offer.

He sniffed. "Can I have a fry-up?"

"No, you cannot have a fry-up," said Clarissa and reached for the can of rabbit and his tub of mixer. It was the same mixer whatever flavour meat she gave him. This seemed unfair to Toby. She wouldn't add boiled potatoes to her curry or her fried fish or lasagne, would she? The least she could do would be to source some *gordon bleugh* accompaniments for his main dish.

Hmpf.

She doled out a quarter of a can of the meat and the same amount of mixer and set it down next to his water bowl. Before he had the chance to twist his nose up and complain, Clarissa reared away from him. "Good grief, Toby! Where have you been?"

Toby stared up at her, confused. "Out," he said.

"Out where?" she demanded.

"Out, out," said Toby. He didn't dare tell her how far he'd wandered because she tended to get a bit cross when she found out about his shenanigans away from home.

And by 'a bit', he meant she went totally ballistic.

"Well, not out in the garden, out," she surmised, leaning over and taking hold of his collar so she could see it better. "Ugh! Ugh! I've got whatever it is on my fingers!" She let go of his collar and raced to the sink to scrub her hands with boiling hot water and washing-up liquid. "Oh my word! Honky!"

Once her hands were pink from the water and she'd rinsed them at least a dozen times, she dried them off on a tea towel and threw it inside the washing machine. Sniffing her fingers, she pulled a face. "Crikey! I can still smell it! What is it? Have you been rolling?"

"I might have had a bit of a roll," Toby admitted. *What a load of fuss!*

"Is it fox? Badger?"

Toby yawned. "I haven't rolled in a fox. Or a badger, come to that. I've never even met a badger. Although I'd love to, if you know of one."

"Fox or badger *poop*!"

Hoomans get so worked up about something so natural, Toby thought. "Maybe I have, I don't recall." He began to munch on the food in his bowl. If this inquisition went on any longer, he'd starve to death.

"I'll go and roll in the grass in a minute," he mumbled, with biscuit in his mouth. "Wipe it off."

"Don't talk with your mouth full." Clarissa washed her hands once more and dried them on a clean tea towel that again found its way directly into the washing machine. As Toby finished his breakfast, his ears twitching to listen to what she was doing, she went into the living room and tapped away on her laptop, her own breakfast forgotten. When the tapping stopped, she disappeared into the hall to use the house phone there. Toby could no longer hear what she was saying, but his stomach got the better of his nosiness so he didn't care.

"Right!" she said, returning a few minutes later. "You're in for a proper treat this morning."

"Am I?" Toby licked his bowl clean. "Sossidge sammich?"

Clarissa sounded far too cheerful. "No, far better than that. In fact, better than any food type you can think of!"

Now this was just absurd. Toby could think of *many* food types that were better than anything else ever in the world. Sossidges, for starters.

"I've booked you in for a spa treatment," Clarissa announced.

Toby frowned. "I'm sorry? A who-y what-y?"

"A spa treatment," she repeated. "It's as much a treat for me as it is for you, for the simple fact that I don't have to put you in the shower and get drenched myself while still ending up smelling like a decomposing seagull."

"Seagull is an interesting scent," Toby admitted. "One of my favourites. But I don't understand." He pondered on her words. "You're sending me off to have a shower somewhere other than here in the house?"

"Yes. I'm paying someone to put you in a bath and make you shiny and sweet-smelling."

Toby frowned. "You're *paying* someone to give me a barf?" *What a ridiculous waste of money!*

"She'll do more than bathe you," Clarissa sang. She seemed wildly enthusiastic about the whole sad affair. "You'll have a hair trim and a nail trim and your ears cleaned and you're ana—hmm—never mind about that."

Never mind about what? Toby cocked his head. What wasn't she telling him? He held up a paw to stop her. "It's okay. You don't need to waste our sammich money. I'm quite happy to have a barf here. I won't wriggle too much," he promised.

"You're looking scruffy," Clarissa said.

"I like scruffy. I'm a scruffy dog. Scruffy dogs are

supposed to look scruffy, otherwise they can't be called scruffy anymore."

"As luck would have it, there's a dog groomer in town that has a cancellation this morning, so we're going to take a walk over there right now."

Toby stepped towards the dog flap. "But I haven't had my post-breakfast nap yet!"

"We're going to have to postpone that for today, I'm afraid." Clarissa moved to block his path.

Toby's shoulders slumped. "How will I have any energy for doing any wizarding this afternoon if I don't get enough rest this morning?"

Clarissa reached out to lock the back door, chuckling. "You know, Toby? I've never known you to be short of energy, so let's not pretend that's actually a possibility." She indicated the hallway where his lead was hanging next to the front door. "Shall we?"

CHAPTER TWO

Toby's bad mood didn't last for long.

By the time he'd set foot outside the front door, he'd forgotten what he'd been grumbling about. He had food in his belly and the day was pleasant enough. The leaves were beginning to change colour but hadn't started to drop yet. Any sort of walk—especially in the company of the hooman he loved—had the potential to be an adventure.

And Toby loved adventures.

He trotted alongside Clarissa, alternately checking his pee-mails and sending his own, or sniffing the bushes or fences or lampposts for anything worth his consideration. When he wasn't sniffing or tugging towards a postbox, he walked beautifully with his little tail up and his chin high. If he could have whistled as he walked, he definitely would have done.

Fortunately for Clarissa, dogs can't whistle.

He greeted the neighbours he met with a wag and a sniff. In fact, he greeted everyone that way, except the poor old postman, but them were the breaks. The postie was probably used to being called out for his stubborn refusal to stay away from the letterbox anyway!

"Do we need to call into the shop?" Toby asked, peering back over his shoulder as they drew closer to the mini-market Clarissa often popped into.

"I need some bread and milk," Clarissa said, "but don't worry, I'll pick that up after I've dropped you off."

Toby pulled up so suddenly that Clarissa almost walked into him and dropped the lead as she fought for balance. "I'm sorry? What did you say?" he asked.

Clarissa scrambled on the ground, fumbling for the end of what Toby referred to as *her* lead. "Which part? Bread and milk?"

"Drop me off?" Toby repeated. "What do you mean, drop me off?"

"Oh, I see." Clarissa straightened up and gave the lead a small tug. "We're going to be late."

"That's not answering my question." Toby dug

his claws into the concrete surface of the paving slabs. He wasn't going anywhere.

Clarissa sighed. "You're impossible sometimes. I have to drop you off. I can't stay *with* you."

"You're not staying with me?" Toby couldn't believe his cute, furry ears.

"It's not the done thing," Clarissa explained. "Groomers don't want owners standing over their shoulder watching their every move."

"But, but—" Toby floundered.

"Jeepers creepers, Tobes. It's not as though you're a scaredy cat. I wouldn't be having to take you to a grooming salon *at all* if you hadn't gone gallivanting around the countryside—*by yourself*, I might add—and given yourself a bath in a wildlife lavatory! Let's not pretend you didn't!"

"That's not the point—"

"It most certainly is the point!" Clarissa shook her head in exasperation. "You don't need me to hold your paw. You're a big boy—"

"I'm still a baby," Toby interrupted. He wasn't. He was nearly two. But it was worth a try.

"You're a grown-assed wizard dog, so stop being daft." Clarissa smiled down at him, not genuinely annoyed. "You'll probably enjoy it, knowing you."

"I doubt it," Toby muttered, but he set off again,

leading Clarissa further into town. On the opposite side of the road, the park called to him. Some of his mates would be playing out. He half considered making a break for it, but he knew Clarissa would kick his backside if he did that. Instead, he reluctantly turned right into the top of Mayflower Lane, a street that led down to the marketplace, keeping an eye out for his friend Pippin in case she smelled him coming.

If she did, she didn't show herself, and all too soon, the pink-and-white striped sun canopy of Sweet Pea's Parlour for Pampered Pooches hove into view. A couple of doors down, the black-and-gold canopy of Goober's the Chemist flapped in the breeze, the queue a moderate six deep.

"That brings back memories, doesn't it?" Toby smiled up at Clarissa. "Maybe we should go and say hello to Deb—"

Clarissa pointed at Sweet Pea's door. "In."

Toby huffed but pushed the door open. Above their heads a cheerful bell jangled, lost beneath the roar of a hairdryer. They stepped into a narrow waiting area with a couple of bright pink bucket seats facing a counter that ran the width of the shop and a tall set of shelves with neatly arranged pet products. Toby lifted his nose and sniffed. His nostrils were met with a warm waft of sweet-scented air: cherries and summer flowers—that would be the products, presumably—and wet dog.

Lovely!

The hairdryer cut off and a woman hurried over. "Hi!" She beamed, peeking over the counter to take a look at Toby. "Hey, buddy!"

"My name's Toby," Toby told her, just in case she thought it *was* Buddy.

Clarissa nudged him with her knee. "I'm Clarissa and this is Toby. I called you earlier."

"That's right!" The woman flipped up part of the counter and unlatched a door, stepping through and securing it after herself.

"Whoa!" Toby was impressed. "Magick!"

"He's a vocal chap, isn't he?" The woman laughed and knelt beside him. Dressed in baggy pink dungarees with a yellow t-shirt underneath, she had a pale, freckled face and pink hair tied up in little bunches on each side of her head. "I'm Peony Shaw," she said, scruggling his head. "You can call me Pea."

"Ah, as in Sweet Pea!" Clarissa observed. "Clever."

Toby strived to remain aloof, but next to sammiches, head scruggles were one of his favourite things. He wagged his back end. "Oooh, yeah. Just there," he said.

"I apologise for the state of him," said Clarissa.

"Had a bit of a roll, has he?" Pea asked, chuckling.

"I deny everything," said Toby.

Clarissa crinkled her nose. "Yes. He's ... erm ... fragrant."

"Don't worry, I'm used to it." Pea stood up. "I just need to get you to fill in a form with all your details, phone number and so on—"

"She's my next of kin," Toby said. "If anything happens to me—"

"Ssh!" Clarissa hissed down at him before smiling at Pea and shrugging. "He's never been to a groomer before."

"Well, you're in for a treat!" Pea reached out and took the lead from Clarissa. "You're going to love it, I promise." She reached over to unlatch her magickal door and led Toby through while Clarissa filled in the form. "Come and meet Pickle."

The other side of the counter was a little different to the front of the shop, but it had a squidgy pink sofa placed against the side wall that matched the bucket chairs, and this is where a poodle had made herself comfortable, curled up among an array of pink cushions and a hand-crocheted blanket in bright colours, predominantly—and this will be of no surprise—different shades of pink. The poodle regarded Toby solemnly but didn't so much as lift her head.

There were a pair of tables—a Border terrier had been secured to one, and he stood there gazing down at Toby with a mixture of dread and fascination—and a huge stainless-steel barf for starters, as well as shelves full of enormous plastic bottles of coloured liquids that must most likely be shampoos and conditioners. On the wall were hooks holding scissors and clippers and combs and brushes and ... well, you name something used to remove bits of dog—in a non-surgical sense—and you'd find it here.

Toby regarded the wall and the range of implements with horror. Could this be some sort of torture chamber? At home, Clarissa used a bog-standard dog shampoo from the local pet shop and that was all. Until Toby had had the foresight to chew it up, she'd often used a comb after his barfs to get the worst of the tangles out, but she hadn't replaced the one he'd destroyed and, in his opinion, a little bit of matting did no harm.

Pea obviously didn't agree. "Oooh, we'll have to get rid of those tats, won't we, Toby?" she trilled, running her fingers through his coat. "Quite thick in places. I bet you were warm this summer."

"Everyone was warm this summer," Toby reminded her. "It was one of the hottest summers on record!"

"Sorry about the matting." On the other side of the counter, Clarissa sounded guilty.

"He's not that bad," Pea said. "I've seen far worse." She took the clipboard from Clarissa. "Let's see. No allergies?"

"No."

"And is this the best number to reach you on?"

"My mobile, yes. I'm going to pick up a few bits of shopping and then head home. How long before I need to come and pick him up?"

"Okay. I have another client in currently ... so ... two, two-and-a-half hours?"

"That's perfect, thank you."

Toby picked out the sound of Clarissa's Dr Marten sandals clopping away from the counter. "Are you leaving already?" he called.

"Back in two hours!" she said.

"But—"

"Bye, Tobes! Missing you already!" The bell jangled as the door opened, then again as it was closed. Clarissa had gone.

Toby stood stock still, ears perky. *She's abandoned me!*

Pea reached down and petted his head. "I promise you'll have a lovely time," she said. "Would you like a treat?"

She fished a couple of bone-shaped biscuits out of her pocket. "Beef, tuna or cheese?"

Clarissa was instantly forgotten. "Cheese, please, Pea," said Toby. "That's my favourite favourite."

CHAPTER THREE

"Interesting," said the poodle on the sofa.

Toby's gaze cut to her. "Pardon me?"

"You chose cheese." She lifted her head and rearranged her paws neatly in front of her chest.

"Was that the wrong thing to do?" Toby asked.

"It's ... *telling*," she said, and lay her chin down once more.

"This is Pickle," Pea told Toby. "She's my girl. Isn't she beautiful?"

Toby appraised the white poodle with her bouffant coat and fluffy ears. She was certainly a looker. Pickle blinked but otherwise didn't react to Pea's obvious pride or Toby's overt scrutiny.

"And these are all of her trophies." Pea gestured at the shelves above the sofa where an array of trophies and gold plaques rubbed shoulders with red and blue rosettes and certificates. "She's a show dog."

"What's a show dog?" Toby asked, but Pea was guiding him into a wooden pen, complete with a blanket and a bowl of water, and she didn't reply.

Neither did Pickle, who appeared to have turned her attention to her beautifully manicured claws.

"Have a little rest there, Toby, while I finish off Nugget. It'll be your turn next."

"Oh, okay," said Toby, sniffing the blanket in case any treats or scraps had been abandoned here. He was out of luck. He scratched at the blanket a few times, turning about again and again until at last he'd made the perfect amount of scrunched-upness and collapsed on top of it. Content for now, he watched as Pea made a beeline for the Border terrier and picked up her pink hairdryer.

"Does everything have to be pink?" Toby asked, imagining that the poodle, aloof as she was, wouldn't deign to answer.

She did, though. "Of course. What's the alternative? Blue?"

"What's wrong with blue?" Toby wanted to know.

"Well, everything. *Der.*"

Toby's eyebrows knitted together. "I don't have anything against pink. I just wondered why—"

The poodle cut him off, raising a paw in his direction. "Boring."

"Oh." Toby was quite taken aback by this. Since when did *anybody* think *he* was *boring*? He fell silent, but only for a few seconds. "Can I just ask—"

"No." The poodle yawned.

Toby pressed on. He simply *had* to know. "Do you think a conversation about colours is boring, or is it that you think *I'm* boring?"

The poodle turned her head and regarded him with complete derision.

"Because, you know, I can't remember the last time I found *anything* boring!"

The poodle seemed to consider this. "Nothing at all?" she asked.

"Nothing at all," Toby confirmed. "I like to learn new things, don't you?"

The poodle remained silent.

"Like"—Toby screwed up his face—"what a show dog does exactly and why pink is better than blue and why taking a cheese treat is 'interesting'."

"Are you always such hard work?" the poodle asked. "Where do you get all the energy? You must drive your owner ragged."

What did 'drive your owner ragged' mean? Clarissa didn't have much money, but they were certainly getting by a little better than they had been when she'd first adopted him. She didn't spend a lot on clothes, just relied on what she had. But the contents of her wardrobe weren't *ragged*. Not yet.

At least he understood the bit about having lots of energy. "I suppose I'm energetic because I get the correct sustenance," said Toby. "Starting with cheese treats." He cocked his head. "Which flavour would you prefer?"

Pickle answered without hesitation. "Tuna. They're lower in fat and better for you. It's important I keep my figure."

"I like tuna," Toby agreed. He liked Pickle's figure too, what he could see of it. He decided not to say so on the grounds that she probably wouldn't appreciate such a comment.

"And yet you chose cheese. The treat of mongrels."

Had Toby heard her correctly? "I beg your pardon?"

"It's a low-class thing," the poodle said.

"I just like the smell. Cheese is stinkier than beef. Tuna comes a close second. I don't think my choice has anything to do with being a crossbreed or a pedigree or a … a …"

"A mongrel," Pickle finished for him. "Which you undoubtedly are."

Toby, more than a little stunned by the poodle's arrogance, lapsed into silence and turned his head away, watching Pea wielding the hairdryer with impressive skill. She teased at Nugget's coarse hair with a comb—pink, of course—and hummed along to an imaginary song.

"Have I hurt your feelings?" The poodle spoke again. She had the air of someone who knows they have but doesn't particularly care.

Toby lifted his chin. "Of course not. I know what I am. I'm a schnauzer-collie-whippet-terrier-thingie, and I'm proud of that."

"That's nice." Pickle tipped her head, raising her eyes towards the shelves holding her trophies. "I can't imagine being you. My whole life revolves around shows and judging and winning things."

"I can't imagine being you and being so *judgy*," said Toby, then bit his tongue. It wasn't right to let Pickle get under his skin. Just because she was choosing to be rude didn't mean that he should respond in a similar vein. Besides, he was pretty sure 'judgy' wasn't a word. He'd have to look it up in his dictionary when he eventually made it home. He cleared his throat and started again. "What is a show dog?"

Perhaps his jibe had hit home. Pickle modulated her tone. "It's a dog who competes at dog shows."

"Ah." Toby remembered the posters he'd seen recently for a dog show that would be held in the park this coming weekend. "So if I enter a dog show, that would make me a show dog?"

"Certainly not!" Pickle scoffed. "Besides, you'd never be allowed to enter. You have to be registered with The Kennel Club, and that means you have to be a pedigree like me." She gestured towards a sizable, framed certificate on the wall by the back door. "Do you see that? That's my family tree! A history of my foremothers and forefathers. Champions and Show Champions, the lot of them—and even a couple of Fluffts Champions of Champions!"

Toby, who didn't have the foggiest notion what The Kennel Club might be, or the slightest clue about his own parentage, or even a passing awareness of Fluffts, wasn't sure that what Pickle was saying was entirely correct. The posters he'd seen had said *Family Fun Dog Show*, which surely insinuated that *all* family dogs could participate? There had been no mention of being able to trace your ancestry back to Roman Britain!

Perhaps that had been in the small print.

He'd have to take another peek at the poster the next time he visited the park.

"It makes me special," Pickle was saying. "What's special about you?" She looked down her nose at him.

"I'm a wizard," he told Pickle.

She rolled her eyes. "I bet you watch too much television."

"Is it actually possible to watch too much television?" Toby asked. "There's so much worth watching—"

"It's making you deluded. Too much *Game of Bones*!" Pickle laughed. "A wizard, my fine furry backside."

"But I am!"

"Ha!" Pickle wrinkled her nose. "Prove it."

"Prove it?" Toby opened and closed his mouth.

"Yes. Show me something magical and mysterious!"

Toby's head swivelled. What could he do that wouldn't draw too much attention from Pea? Clarissa had drummed into him that, as far as possible, he should hide his skills from the mundane population. Magick was none of their business. Especially if they didn't believe in it or they didn't want to engage with it.

Their loss, as far as Toby was concerned, but Clarissa was boss.

He considered squirting shampoo from the enormous bottle located next to the stainless-steel bath, but that would certainly alert Pea. He could scatter Pea's collection of scissors and combs and brushes from the table beside her, but Pickle might blame that on Pea if she didn't see it and, again, Pea would wonder what had happened.

Toby settled on the wooden back door painted the same shade of pink as most of the parlour's accessories. He could see the chunky iron hoop of the back end of the key in the lock.

Toby turned to Pickle. "Watch the key," he ordered, then lifted a paw. "*Ob-tor-key-o*!" The key turned smoothly, and something in the mechanism clicked.

Pickle evidently heard it because her ears twitched, but she said nothing.

"*Open*," said Toby, concentrating his energy on the handle. The handle rattled but the door remained closed. "Was the door unlocked?" Toby asked. "I'd assumed it wasn't."

"Pea usually leaves it unlocked while she's in the shop. She goes in and out to the rubbish bins in the yard."

"Ah. That makes sense." Toby concentrated again. "*Recludo.*" He unlocked the door. "*Ob-tor-key-o*!" The mechanism clicked. He concentrated on the handle. This time when he wiggled it, it sprang open.

Before he had a chance to close it again, Pea glanced up. "Oooh!" She hurried over and pulled the door wide. "Anyone there?" she called, looking out into the yard. Satisfied there was no-one hiding, she shut the door and this time locked it herself. "Must have been the wind," she muttered.

Pickle raised her immaculately sculpted eyebrows. "Mmm," she said. Nothing more.

The bell jangling at the shop entrance interrupted them.

Pickle placed her head on her paws and closed her eyes, completely disinterested in the goings-on. In contrast, Toby reared up on his hind legs, trying to see. The counter was too high, so he couldn't, but Nugget, still attached to the grooming table, had started to wag his stumpy tail so fast it became a blur.

"Perfect timing!" called Pea and began to detach Nugget from his harness.

"Has he been a good boy?" an unseen lady crooned.

"Of course! He's always a superstar," said Pea, and unlatched her magick gate in order to hand Nugget over. There was an exchange of further pleasantries, more cooing and the sound of a till ringing, the beep of the card machine and the whir of a printer. "See you in six weeks!" called Pea, and the bell jangled again.

"Smashing," said Pea to no-one in particular, and began sweeping up around the grooming table. Once she'd disposed of the hair and fluff, she turned to beam at Toby. "Let's get you in the bath, shall we?"

"Try not to drown," said Pickle, opening her eyes but without looking his way.

Toby cast a sideways glance at the poodle. "I can swim," he told her. "Can you?"

Pickle's eyes widened. "I've never felt the need to do so," she told him, lifting her haughty nose.

"Ah!" Toby grinned triumphantly. "So you don't know whether you can or you can't!"

"If *you* can, it can't be that difficult." Pickle turned her head so that she wasn't looking at him.

Pea picked Toby up. "That's quite a conversation you two are having," she remarked. "Are you flirting?"

"Flirting?" Toby sputtered. "Not on your life!"

"Beautiful, isn't she?" Pea enthused, not having a clue what Toby was saying. She gently lowered Toby into a wonderfully warm and sweetly scented tub of soapy water. "My pride and joy!"

Toby lifted his head. "Beautiful she may be, but by dog, she's the most insufferable pooch I ever had the misfortune to meet!"

"There, there," cooed Pea, mistaking his grumbles. "There, there."

CHAPTER FOUR

"Oh I do like to be beside the parkside ..." Toby sang as he and Clarissa entered the park on Saturday morning. Feeling chipper, he had his nose in the air and skipped happily along beside Clarissa and Not-so-dead-to-me Ed.

"It's busy here today," said Ed, looping his arm through Clarissa's.

Toby aimed a little stink-eye Ed's way, but not too much because he'd decided that the young DC Plum was a whole lot better for Clarissa than ninety-nine point nine nine nine nine nine nine per cent of the available alternatives.

"It looks like there's a dog show on," said Clarissa, pointing at one of the posters. "It's drawing quite a crowd."

Toby smiled smugly to himself. He knew all about the dog show, of course. After the conversation with Pickle a few days earlier, he'd insisted Clarissa walk home via the park when she came to pick him up. He'd diligently read the small print, and it said nothing at all either about The Kennel Club or about having to prove descendance from Neanderthal wolves. There were a few pedigree classes—that's what he'd learned, that there were lots of different classes you could enter—but most of the show was dedicated to family dogs.

He and Clarissa were a family. Right?

While Clarissa and Ed stopped to chat with someone they recognised, Toby ambled towards a clutch of tents and stalls. These flanked a pair of sizable show rings, demarcated by iron rods stuck into the grass, with plastic ribbons tied around the tops to form the boundaries. Even when Clarissa called him back, he nonchalantly took a few more steps closer.

Clarissa hurried after him and clipped the lead to his collar. "So many dogs!" she marvelled. "It's probably better if we keep you close."

"We should enter Toby in the show," said Ed, catching them up.

Clarissa, much to Toby's consternation, guffawed. "Seriously?"

"Why not?" Ed nodded approvingly down at Toby. "He looks handsome after his pampering the other day."

"Attaboy." Toby mentally put a tick next to Ed's name. "At this rate, you won't be dead to me at all, Eddie, my friend."

"I suppose he does." Clarissa curled her lip. "I don't know, though ... he's not a pedigree. Aren't dog shows for posh dogs?"

"Not always. Let's have a look at the classes, shall we? Wait here!" Ed scurried off towards a table in the first tent on their left. A big sign above proclaimed *REGISTRATION*.

Clarissa dropped her gaze to Toby. "Would you be interested in entering?" she asked him, sounding doubtful. "You don't have to if you don't want to."

Toby, slightly taken aback by her lack of enthusiasm for his evident good looks, gave her his best ten-yard stare.

"That's what I thought," said Clarissa, misconstruing his meaning. "Let's find Ed—"

Toby cleared his throat. "I'm sure I can have a crack at it," he said, trying not to sound too eager. "I mean, it can't be that difficult, can it?" He thought of Pickle and her arrogance. How dare she suggest he—a great wizard-in-waiting—couldn't make it as a show dog.

"Really?" Clarissa sounded surprised. "Here's Ed. Let's see what he's found out."

Ed hurried up to them, smiling and waving an A5-sized poster. "This has a list of classes," he said. "Just as I thought, it's only a fun show. There are a couple of classes for pedigrees, but most of them are for all dogs so we can enter Toby in a few. It'll be a laugh!"

Toby wrinkled his nose, staring up at Ed. What was this 'laugh' business? Couldn't he see that Toby was deadly serious?

"What sort of classes are there?" Clarissa snuggled up next to Ed and they pored over the information together.

"Don't mind me," Toby muttered.

"Is there one for Grumpiest Dog?" Clarissa asked Ed.

He laughed. "Most Handsome Boy. We have to enter him for that."

Toby nodded. "Absolutely we do."

"There are lots of novelty classes. What about Best Biscuit Catcher?" Ed suggested.

Toby pricked his ears up. "I could certainly have

a go." Even if he didn't win, the perks would be worth it!

"Maybe," said Clarissa. "He'd win if we were throwing sammiches at him."

"We could practise if you like?" Toby could smell a burger van close by. *Nom nom nom.*

"What about Best Rescue?" Ed wanted to know.

Clarissa shook her head. "I'm not sure we can class him as a rescue dog. He belonged to my grandad."

"I rescued you," Toby pointed out to Clarissa. "Maybe you should enter."

"Ssh." She nudged him with her toe. "Oh, look. Here's a perfect one. Best Trick!"

Ed peered down at Toby. "Can you do a trick?"

Toby did a double take. *What?* "I'm a trainee wizard, Ed! Of course I can do tricks. Why, just a few weeks ago I conjured dozens of skeletons—"

Clarissa hurried to interrupt him. "You know, on second thoughts, let's not enter that class."

"Spoilsport," said Ed and Toby at the same time.

"Most Handsome Boy seems our best bet," Clarissa decided.

"Or this one? Best Eyebrows?"

Clarissa guffawed. "No way! Really?"

"Absolutely!" Ed laughed along with her.

"Classes are one pound fifty for the first one and a pound for every additional one, so I might as well put him in for Most Handsome Boy, Best Eyebrows and Best Biscuit Catcher."

Clarissa reached into her handbag for her purse.

"My treat," said Ed, and headed off to the registration tent to sign Toby up.

"You really should have let me enter Best Trick," Toby said, standing on Clarissa's toes.

"You have to be joking. I don't even want to think about what you'd do!"

"I could levitate the judge," Toby suggested. "Or—"

"Oh, look!" Clarissa changed the subject. "There's Pea with Pickle. Come on. Let's say hello." She shot sideways. Toby, on the other end of Clarissa's lead, had no choice but to go with her. They didn't have to go far before he found himself face to face with Pickle.

"Hi again," he said brightly.

Pickle took a step away from him. "Oh, it's you."

"You look mighty fine," Toby told her. And she did. Pea certainly knew how to dress Pickle for success. Pickle had been poofed and preened with precision, her white fur shining and teased to glorious perfection. She sported a matching leather collar-and-lead set—pink, of course—with Swarovski diamanté sparkles, all in marked contrast to Toby's cheap fabric collar with bone decoration and Clarissa's mismatching lead in blue rope.

"I know," said Pickle and turned her face away.

Above their heads, Clarissa and Pea were exchanging pleasantries. "Are you entering Toby?" Pea was asking. Today she had forgone the dungarees and was instead wearing a bright pink sundress with enormous white triangular buttons, teamed with thick-soled trainers. "He's such a cutie."

"In a couple of classes," Clarissa admitted. "But it's just for fun. We're not serious like you are."

Pea laughed. "Pickle loves it. Or should I say, Pickford's Afterglow." Clarissa must have looked confused because Pea added, "Pickford's Afterglow is her Kennel Club name. I shorten it to Pickle, but on show day, she has to be addressed correctly. She insists."

Pickle turned her head up to smile winningly at Clarissa. "I do."

"Do you have any tips for us?" Clarissa asked.

Pea nodded. "Try and encourage Toby to look at the judge as much as possible and get him to stand in such a way the judge can see his form properly. Then, when you're asked to move around the ring, try a little running. The judges love to see the movement, and Toby will be less likely to sniff the ground—"

"Or stop for a wee—" Clarissa chuckled.

"Exactly!" Pea grinned. "Anyway, we'd best go and register. Good luck!"

"Thanks. You too!" Clarissa called after them.

Toby turned to observe Pickle move. She certainly was elegant, placing her paws daintily on the ground, and keeping her head up and her ears perky.

Pffft! thought Toby. *Anyone can do that.*

As Clarissa led him off in search of Ed, Toby practised arranging each paw delicately in front of the other and stretching his head up.

"What are you doing?" Clarissa asked, slowing her pace so he could catch up. "Stop messing around!"

That's nice, isn't it? thought Toby. *Maybe I'll never be a show dog simply because Clarissa doesn't fully appreciate my amazingness!* "I'm practising my skillz," he told her.

"Well, can you do it a little faster?" Clarissa suggested, hurrying him along. "I'm falling over my own feet here."

"Maybe you'd better practise *your* footwork,"

Toby said. "Or you'll be the one falling over your feet in the ring, and we don't want that."

Clarissa peered down at him. "You do know we're doing this for *fun*, right, furry boy?"

"Absolutely! Totally!" Toby agreed.

But secretly, he knew better. *Over my dead body*, he thought. *I've totally got this!*

CHAPTER FIVE

It turned out that Toby was far from being Sun Valley's Best Biscuit Catcher. He finished over halfway down the field, way behind the winning Staffy, who'd been a demon snaffler, and the second-placed Jack Russell-cross-bichon-frise-cross-anonymous-rescue-hound.

"Phooey," Toby complained to Ed.

Ed, who had almost bust a gut, he'd laughed so much as Toby leapt and pranced and tried to catch the judge's biscuits, wiped his eyes. "I think you need more practice, Toby!"

"I'm game if you are," Toby assured him. "There are some stalls over there where you can buy home-made treats. Perhaps we could indulge?"

Clarissa was waiting for them as they exited the

ring. "We need to go over to the bigger ring," she said. "Most Handsome Boy is coming up soon."

Ed pulled the timetable of classes out of his pocket. It had started to look crumpled now, it had been consulted so often. "There's no clash with Best Eyebrows, is there?"

"No!" Clarissa laughed and tugged at his arm. "You've checked that a dozen times! Who knew you were such a worrier?"

They found a space on the perimeter of the second ring—the bigger of the two—so they could watch proceedings. This was an eye-opener for all of them because they'd never really seen how classes such as this were conducted.

Inside this ring, the judge, an older gentleman with soft white hair covered by a flat cap and a matching tweed jacket, was overseeing the Best Pedigree Bitch class. To be fair, the class wasn't that large. There were a pair of golden retrievers, a beagle, a German shepherd, a husky, a Chihuahua, a Pekingese and a bichon frise, but for the most part, the dogs attending the show were cuddly crossbreeds and family rescues accompanied by excited little munchkins and their parents, huddling around the barriers to watch a canine form of class warfare play out.

"They think they're better than us," one dachshund-cross-something that might have been related to a yellow Labrador complained.

"They wouldn't get very far in a fist fight," a boxer-come-furry-something said. "They're no better than anyone!"

"And besides which," a chunky labradoodle with a thick curly coat chipped in, "everyone knows pedigree dogs are more prone to ailments. They have *nothing* to feel superior about."

"That's right, that's right," several other dogs muttered.

"Peace and love, peace and love," Toby called. He'd started channelling positive energy and good thoughts, hoping he could transfer those to the judge.

"Oh my life, we have a hippie in our midst," grumbled the boxer-come-furry-something.

"Hey, Toby!" the dachshund called. "Is that you?"

"It is. Hi, Freddo!" Toby recognised the voice, if not the dog. He'd realised that there were dozens and dozens of dogs here that he was acquainted with, if not in person then through the Twilight Barking. "How are you doing?"

"I'm good." Freddo pulled on his lead to get a

little slack from his owner so he could come over and bump noses. "Are you entering anything?"

"A couple of things," Toby admitted. "But just for fun." He repeated the age-old lie. "What about you?"

"I entered the Dog Who Most Resembles Their Owner and we won a yellow rosette!"

"Congratulations!" Toby glanced up at Freddo's owner. She had a thatch of straw-like yellow hair that very much mirrored her pup's fur. "What does a yellow rosette signify?"

Freddo giggled. "I have no idea, but I like it!"

There were a couple of oohs from the dogs around them. Toby turned his attention back to the ring. Pickle had just entered with Pea and taken her place in the line-up. The lady owner of the German shepherd glowered at them, and the gentleman with the beagle blew out his cheeks and shook his head.

"She's the real deal," said the labradoodle.

"Perfection," the boxer agreed.

It turned out the judge agreed. After all nine dogs had been inspected—tails lifted, teeth and gums exposed, backbone felt—and they'd all walked—or trotted—around the ring a couple of times, the rosettes were handed out. A yellow for the

Pekingese, a blue for the bichon frise and the red for Pickle.

There was a smattering of polite applause.

"That was the obvious result straight from the get-go, huh?" Freddo said, and Toby had to agree. Pickle had the grace, the elegance and the looks. She moved beautifully. If she hadn't been such a mean old cow, he'd probably be in love with her.

Close by, the nearest tannoy began its distorted booming. "The next class in ring two is the Most Handsome Boy. This is an open class for all breeds aged one year and over. Please make your way to the ring ..."

"Oooh, Toby, that's us!" Clarissa shrieked, a little too loudly.

Toby grimaced. "She's a little over-excited. I do apologise," he told his friends.

"First time?" the boxer asked.

"And probably the last," Toby said, and let Clarissa lead him towards ring two where she gave Toby's name and registration number to the woman waiting there. The official—she must have been official because she was wearing a lanyard—crossed them off the list on her clipboard and directed them to take a position in a circle.

Where the previous class had numbered nine

dogs, in this class, there were ... Toby did a rough headcount ... fifty-two.

Fifty-two!

"Ohmyword," Clarissa said. "Toby, we don't stand a chance!"

"Never say never!" said Toby, but even he had started having second thoughts. The mix of dogs—of all ages, all shapes and sizes—was quite something. Added to this, the pedigree boys were also permitted to participate. A particularly fine red setter already stood out from the crowd, given his colouring and the shine on his glorious coat.

A plump Yorkie-cross-Highland-terrier next to Toby began to sing. "If I were an Afghan, yah-dadadadadadadadadadadadadadaaaaaah! All day long I wouldn't have to *werk*, if I were an Afghan hound!"

"Oi!" shouted a couple of Toby's neighbours, and they all fell about laughing.

The atmosphere was one of excitement and chaos. The official, clutching her clipboard and her rosettes, did her best to line everyone up—but it was a bit like herding cats, except with dogs, and an awful lot of woofing and yowling and a few growls.

Eventually there was some semblance of order,

and the judge—the same one from the pedigree class—took a quick walk around.

"Don't forget to look at the judge," Clarissa whispered to Toby, but there was no need. Toby had learned from observing Pickle. He copied, to the best of his ability, her stance. Neck stretching, chin up, legs perfectly angled, chest out, belly in, ears perky.

The judge completed his circuit and then asked the person at the front of the line to walk around.

"Man! This is going to take forever!" complained the plump Yorkie, and promptly collapsed onto the ground for a nap.

Toby wasn't sure whether to relax or not. If the judge looked his way and he was slouched like a skateboarding teenager in the park on a Saturday afternoon, what then? Would he have blown his chances? He decided to remain poised to the best of his ability, although this began to wear thin far more quickly than he'd imagined it would.

Especially when he felt the beginning of an itch below his chin.

"Mind over matter. Mind over matter." His front right paw performed a little tap dance on the grass. "Control, Toby!" Taking a deep breath, he imagined a backscratcher—like the one Old Joe used to have, a kind of extendable fork that you could slip down the back of your shirt to reach a part of your back you otherwise couldn't get to—being wielded by a helpful assistant, Clarissa perhaps, scratching gently away at his beard. *Mmmmm.* He closed his eyes. *Heavenly.*

"He's very chilled, isn't he?"

Toby opened his eyes to find the judge peering down at him.

"Sometimes." Clarissa laughed. She sounded nervous.

"Always," said Toby.

"A schnauzer cross, is he?"

"Yes. Schnauzer-whippet-something or other," Clarissa said.

Toby opened his mouth to provide his whole ancestry—what he knew of it—but Clarissa arched an eyebrow at him. *Fair enough.*

"May I?" the judge asked, and knelt beside Toby. Quick as you like he felt along Toby's back, up into his hindquarters, checked in his ears, examined his gums and teeth and turned Toby's head to look at his eyes.

What about my bodily autonomy? Toby wondered. *You can't just manhandle me like this!*

"If you could do a circuit for me, please?" the judge asked Clarissa. "As best you can. I know it's a little crowded."

Clarissa nodded and took off, as light on her feet as possible, bearing in mind Pea's advice to move quickly. Toby obliged by hurrying alongside her. They returned, Clarissa breathless, to their place in the line. The judge nodded and moved on.

"Phew," said Clarissa. "Glad I'm not wearing heels."

"You never wear heels," Toby pointed out. "How do you think I did?"

"I think we did okay. We'll have to wait and see. There are lots of handsome dogs here, though. It's a stiff competition."

Toby had to agree. It had been much easier, surely, for Pickle to finish first in class, given that she had been one of only nine. Every male dog within a ten-mile radius must have been participating in Toby's class. Nonetheless, Toby continued to hold his head up high and keep an eye on the judge.

After what seemed to be an interminably long time, the dog last in line completed his circuit. The judge walked around the circle once more, stopping to stare long and hard at certain dogs.

"This is so much more nerve-wracking than I imagined it would be," said Clarissa.

"You should try being me," said Toby.

The judge pointed at a dog and the owner moved

forward. There was a cheer and applause from the watching crowd. Then another dog. Then another.

"Wait a minute!" Toby grumbled as the judge walked past him. "You've missed me!"

As though the judge had heard him, he back-tracked and indicated Clarissa should step out.

Two more dogs were pulled out into the line, then the judge smiled at the organising lady. She stepped forward with a handful of rosettes including green, pink and purple as well as red, blue and yellow.

"I think we've won a rosette," Clarissa murmured out of the side of her mouth.

The judge walked down the line and handed Clarissa a yellow rosette, shook her hand and patted Toby before moving on.

"Oh my!" Clarissa hopped with excitement. "You came third, Toby!"

Toby couldn't fathom what had gone wrong. "Third? That's an outrage!"

Clarissa danced excitedly in place. "I can't believe it!"

"Neither can I!" Toby grumbled and pulled her from the ring.

Clarissa had pinned the rosette to her denim jacket.

"I'm not sure you should wear that," Ed said, sucking mustard from his fingers. The three of them had celebrated Toby's win with a hot dog. This had provided some consolation to Toby, of course, but he'd come to the conclusion that the judge was partially sighted at best and completely devoid of common sense at worst. He licked his emotional wounds at the same time as the ketchup on his hot dog tray.

"Why not?" Clarissa asked. "I earned it."

"Strictly speaking, Toby earned it." Ed grinned. "But I'm more concerned that it looks like I've won third prize in the girlfriend competition."

Clarissa's mouth dropped open. "Excuse me?"

Ed guffawed and Toby, unable to help himself, joined in.

"I can't believe you just said that," Clarissa said, reaching to unpin the rosette.

"I was only kidding." Ed closed his fingers over hers to stop her from undoing it.

She peeked up through her eyelashes. "Did you just refer to me as your girlfriend?" she asked, suddenly shy.

Ed cocked his head to one side. "I might have done."

"Oh, please!" Toby pretended to cough up his hot dog.

"Is that alright with you?" Ed asked, for a moment looking like a sixteen-year-old boy, his face pale and his cheeks flushed.

Clarissa pretended to think, then she nodded, her eyes lighting up. "Yes," she said. "I think that's perfectly acceptable."

"Yeah. If you two could stop that, that would be great!" Toby called. "We're in public here, you know?"

The tannoy crackled. "The next class in ring one is for Best Eyebrows. This is an open class for all dogs. Please make your way to the ring ..."

"Oh!" Clarissa hurriedly swallowed. "That's us again." She waved her half-eaten hot dog around.

"Do you want me to take him in?" Ed asked.

Clarissa smirked. "Why not? I bet you can't do better than me!"

"I bet I can," said Ed, reaching out to wipe a smudge of tomato ketchup from her chin.

"We'll see!" Clarissa gleefully chomped on her hot dog and waved them both away.

"Come on, fella," Ed whispered down to Toby. "I need to level the score here."

"Excuse me," Toby complained as Ed followed

him to ring one. "It's me who's doing all the work here. I don't think you two realise! *I'm* the one winning, not you two!"

"Oh, hello again!" The lady at the entrance beamed down at Toby. "You've come back, have you?" She checked off Toby's name and number on her list and gestured to the edge of the ring. Toby knew the score; he pulled Ed around until they tagged on to the end of a ragged queue.

This was a much smaller field, only six dogs in total. A Border terrier again, which may or may not have been the same one—Nugget, was it?—he'd first come across in Sweet Pea's Parlour for Pampered Pooches. An Old English sheepdog who didn't have eyebrows so much as fluff sprouting out of every pore. A particularly scruffy and hairy collie-cross-lurcher whose face was a mix of black, grey and white and whose eyebrows wiggled around as he watched the comings and goings around them. A Labrador retriever with a pretty face but no real eyebrows to speak of. And a Yorkshire terrier with interesting tufts above his eyes that rather matched his owner's.

"This is looking good," Ed said. "We have a three in five chance of winning a rosette, so let's hope we get one that's at least as good as Clarissa's."

Spotting the judge entering the ring, Toby nudged Ed's calf with his rump. "Pay attention, Ed. We need to concentrate!" He angled himself towards the judge to give him a good look at his face. Such direct eye contact worked a treat. The judge glanced over at him before turning his attention to the Border terrier.

Toby quickly considered the other dogs. By his reckoning, the lurcher was his biggest competition. He momentarily contemplated sabotaging the lurcher's chances, perhaps by singeing his fur, but that would have been cruel—and besides, the lurcher seemed pretty gormless, more interested in watching a woman spectator eat a toffee apple than wiggling his eyebrows for the judge.

Then there was a possibility that the judge preferred quirky, in which case he'd be tempted by the Yorkshire terrier. But at the end of the day, there's no pride in winning by cheating, so instead Toby funnelled positive thoughts into his soul. "I am beautiful. I am gorgeous. I am a winner," he repeated. "I am beautiful. I am gorgeous. I am a winner!"

The lurcher shied away from the judge, the great woosy thing, but the Labrador retriever put on a decent enough display.

And then it was Toby's turn. "Werk it," he told himself, gazing up at the judge as though the older man was the most beautiful being he had ever seen, filling his eyes with soft, chocolate love and then, when he thought the judge had been sucked in far enough, he twitched his eyebrows.

Being part schnauzer, Toby had been blessed with a fascinating face—he would say a perfect face—and eyebrows that contrasted beautifully with the rest of his facial fur. Whereas for the most part his face was black and grey, his eyebrows were white, rather like Old Joe's had been—big, bushy and white—and they stood out like the headlights on a train.

That was enough for the judge, and seconds later Toby was the proud owner of a bright red rosette. He skipped out of the ring, tail high, leading a jubilant Ed back to a giggling Clarissa.

Put that on your rosette stand, Pickle! Toby thought. *I'm a show dog, too!*

CHAPTER SIX

Basking in the glory of a yellow *and* a red rosette, Toby insisted Clarissa attach both to his collar like he'd seen Pea do for Pickle. Clarissa, Ed and Toby spent the next hour meandering around the park and perusing the stalls, buying a few tombola tickets—they won a can of Branston baked beans and a bar of Cadbury's Dairy Milk—and Ed bought Toby some natural treats from an organic pet food stall.

Toby placed another tick in the Ed box.

After that, they strolled a little further into the park so that Toby could have a run off lead with a few of his friends—although he was mindful of his rosettes, of course, and went nowhere near the duck pond—while Clarissa and Ed sat on a bench drinking coffee from paper cups.

All too soon it was time to leave. Ed was working a late shift, which meant he had to head back and get changed, and Clarissa had to return home to continue working on her latest article for *The Celestine Times*.

And Toby? Well, Toby fancied a nap.

They bid goodbye at the entrance to the park. Toby averted his eyes and took great interest in the nearest bush while Clarissa and Ed spent a little time goodbying. When that had finally been accomplished and Ed hurried back to his car, Clarissa and Toby turned for home.

"Oh, wait!" Clarissa pulled to a sudden stop. "I meant to buy some onions."

Toby wrinkled his nose. He wasn't allowed onions. Apparently, they were poisonous for dogs. This was a blow. He thought they always smelled rather delicious when they were being cooked. Mmmm ... the scent of fried onions ... yum. Or stews or pies. He'd once snuck a piece of raw onion that had fallen on the floor in the kitchen, but it hadn't been at all nice.

Bleurgh!

"Thinking about it, I could do with a few vegetables." Clarissa hesitated. The convenience store they used was only across the road, but sometimes the vegetables could be a bit hit-and-miss. "Shall we walk down to the market?"

"Sounds good to me!" Toby agreed, ever hopeful that he'd run into his best mate, Pippin.

They waited at the pelican crossing until it was safe, Toby enjoying the attention of several teenage girls admiring his rosettes, Clarissa checking her phone on the off chance something exciting had occurred that she'd need to report on for *The Celestine Times*. Ever since zombies had run riot in Sun Valley, Clarissa had seen an increase in work opportunities. Her editor had been sending more scoops Clarissa's way, and she'd been in demand for podcasts and radio interviews.

Toby wasn't remotely unhappy about this. They had more income than previously—which meant higher quality sammich fillings, although cheese would most likely always be one of his most favourite favourites—and they could pay the household bills. If Clarissa was happy, Toby was happy.

The green man appeared, so Toby skipped across the crossing in time to the beep. Clarissa, almost pulled off balance because she hadn't been paying attention, hurriedly stuffed her phone away. They began to stroll along Mayflower Lane towards the market. At this time of the afternoon, the town had quietened. The florist had started to pack up, and the price of the day's leftover flowers had been reduced. Clarissa paused before succumbing to temptation and paying for a bunch of bright sunflowers. She tucked them under her arm, humming happily to herself.

Toby studied her, the flush of her cheeks. Either she was getting the flu or—

Oh. It hit him.

Love.

She was in love.

He'd seen it on the telly. Heard about it in songs. Stupid Cupid shooting his poisonous arrow and severing the strings to the heart. Or something like that.

In love with Not-so-dead-to-me Ed.

Toby checked in on his emotions. *Hmmm. A bit of jealousy brewing there.* Clarissa had been his and his alone for a long time. Some sadness too, because now he wouldn't be Clarissa's one and only. But joy as well because Clarissa was happy.

He wagged his tail and she scruggled his head. "Onwards, McWoof," she ordered, and off he trotted.

Up ahead, towards the end of the lane, Goober's

the Chemist was closed. The sun canopy had been stored away and there was no queue. They closed early on a Saturday and reopened bright and early on Monday morning, when the whole of Sun Valley descended on the business in desperate need of life-saving medicines. Or paracetamol and honey linctus, at any rate.

At the end of the lane, someone was playing a didgeridoo. The deep dirge vibrated in Toby's ears and he shuddered, pulling Clarissa to the side, hoping she'd take a wide berth. They found themselves outside Sweet Pea's Parlour for Pampered Pooches, the pink-and-white striped canopy still casting shade over the pavement.

The door stood ajar. Toby glanced casually inside as they made their way past, wondering if Pickle had arrived home and whether she'd won any other rosettes. Something—some metallic scent—stopped him in his tracks.

Clarissa, who'd carried on walking, was yanked back. "Toby!"

"Uh-oh," he said.

"What's the matter?" She stared down at him, her forehead creasing.

"I smell death," he said.

Clarissa straightened up, glancing around. "You smell death?"

"Yes."

"Where?" She sounded nervous now.

Toby lifted his snout. "Close."

"You know you swore blind you smelled death once before, but Mrs Crouch was alive and kicking!"

"I don't think she was kicking," Toby contradicted Clarissa. "That's not something she does even when she's well."

"Alright, Smarty-pants."

"I'm just saying." Toby snuck a little closer to the open door of Sweet Pea's Parlour for Pampered Pooches. "It's coming from here."

"Oh, cripes. I hope you're wrong." Clarissa swallowed, edging towards the door. "Pea?" she called. "Pea? Are you there?"

Toby barked. "Yo, Pickle?"

"Is there anyone there?" Clarissa asked, craning her head to try and peer inside.

They were met with silence.

Clarissa took a breath. "Why is the door open if there's no-one here?"

"I told you—"

"Yes! I know! You can smell death!" Clarissa cringed. She stepped inside, kicking something pink that clattered away into the corner, making her jump. "It might just be a break-in," she whispered, gathering herself, then called out again, more loudly this time. "Hellooooo?"

Toby followed her. The hair on the back of his neck prickled. Something wasn't right.

Clarissa leaned over the counter to get a better look at the other side, then sharply recoiled, dropping the sunflowers as she did so. "Oh dear! Someone's on the floor. I think it's Pea!"

Dropping the lead, she fumbled with the hatch, finally sliding the lock across and pushing the door open. She hurried through, Toby on her heels, and knelt next to the woman on the floor. She wore bright red dungarees with a white t-shirt and had a scarf knotted in her hair. Toby sidled around a pool of blood, being careful not to slip or get his paws in it. "Pea?" Clarissa cried, placing two fingers against the pulse in the woman's neck. "Oh no, oh no, oh no." Clarissa began hunting for her phone. "Where did I put it? Where is it?" Her voice shook.

Toby glanced over at the sofa. Empty. There were no dogs in the cages either, but white fur lay scattered on the grooming table and around the floor. Had Pea been grooming Pickle when she was attacked? If so, where was Pickle?

But why would Pea have been grooming Pickle when she was already primped to perfection for the dog show?

Toby studied the woman lying prone beside Clarissa. He couldn't see the whole of the woman's face, but of what he could see ... while there was a certain resemblance ...

"I don't think this is Pea," he announced.

Clarissa, in too much of a panic to take in what he was saying, waved him away. "Police!" she was saying. "And ambulance! No. I can't find a pulse. No, she's not breathing. Hurry! Hurry!"

Toby began sniffing around, trying to identify the diverse array of scents. The fragrances of the shampoos and conditioners were the top notes, but there were middle and low notes too, much as any hooman would discern in a perfume factory. An undercurrent of floor-cleaning fluid—something lemony—and polish used on the wooden counter. A wisp of coffee and chocolate. A gentle breath of mint. The more Toby concentrated, the more he could see the layers of scent forming separate air puddles. Light and dusky near the ceiling, warmer towards the tiled floor. The sinks pulsated with strongly scented pink odours, and the sofa gave off a powdered whiff of vanilla and damp dog.

But there were other scents. Hooman ones. Pea, for sure, and now he was certain that the lady on the floor was not Pea. This lady had her own scent, something similar, but spicier than Pea's sweetness. He could identify a muskier scent too. Definitely male. Perspiration. Cigarettes. Chicken flavour crisps and a Coca-Cola. And another woman. Expensive perfume, something slightly old-fashioned. Hairspray and white-linen flavoured deodorant.

Of course, there were other hoomans. These were only the freshest scents. He could have built up an FBI profile of hoomans who'd visited Pea's parlour over the past few weeks.

The back door stood open, allowing a gentle breeze to sweep through the premises.

"Mayflower Lane," Clarissa was saying, sounding tense. "Sweet Pea's Poodle Parlour or whatever it's called."

Toby sniffed along the skirting boards. *Hmmm.* There was a definite scent of rodents here. He followed the boards around until he came to a gap between the floorboards and the skirting boards. "Hello?" he called.

He heard a scuffling noise, swiftly followed by a hissed, "Sssssshhh!" and then silence.

"Hello?" he repeated.

"Who are you talking to, Toby?" Clarissa asked.

Toby frowned at the gap in the floorboards. "Nobody, apparently." He lay down on his haunches and tried to peer into the hole. He thought he saw whiskers.

"We have to go and wait for the police outside," Clarissa said, her voice thick with emotion. "Be careful not to disturb anything."

"Is Ed coming?" Toby asked as he edged around the perimeter of the room, giving the corpse a wide berth.

"I shouldn't have thought so. He won't have started work yet. He was going home first." She pulled the little hatch door closed after him, then opened it again, unsure what to do for the best.

They stood outside, under the sun canopy. "I shouldn't have thought they'd be long," Clarissa said. "It's not as though murders are ten a penny in Sun Valley." She laughed, a sound so hollow she might have been sitting at the bottom of a dry well. Toby gazed up at his beloved hooman, her face pale, her hands shaking. He snuggled next to her calves, hoping he could warm her up and offer a little comfort. "So awful," she said. "Poor Pea."

"It wasn't P—" Toby began, but was interrupted by the arrival of none other than Pea and Pickle.

"Hey!" Pea beamed at them, waving a gold trophy in their direction. Pickle pranced along beside her, two red rosettes and a red-and-gold rosette attached to her collar. She graced Toby with a little side-eye. "Guess who won best in show?" Pea asked.

Clarissa recoiled in horror. "Oh, heavens!"

"Are you alright?" Pea's grin faded, replaced by a look of concern. She joined them under the sun canopy. "Is Toby alright?"

Clarissa fumbled for the right words. "Yes, erm ... The police are coming."

"The police?"

"I thought it was you—"

Pea looked from Clarissa to the shop, spotting the open door. "What's going on?"

Clarissa came to her senses and reached out to grab Pea's wrist. "You mustn't go in there."

"What are you talking about? Where's my sister?"

"Your sister?" Clarissa asked, her voice choking. "Oh, Pea. I'm so sorry!"

"You're sorry?" Pea began to pull free. "What do you mean?"

As Clarissa fought for the words to explain, a

police car, blue lights flashing, sped down Mayflower Lane towards them, pedestrians scattering as it came. Another followed within seconds.

Toby could only watch as proceedings speedily unrolled. One police officer came over to Pea and Clarissa. Clarissa tried to explain. Pea's knees gave way and the officer caught her. A female police officer came over to help, while her partner entered the shop. An ambulance arrived and the paramedics rushed inside. Shoppers began to gather around, wanting to know what was going on. They were pushed back as blue-and-white tape was rolled out to cordon off the crime scene. Pickle stood by, staring at the gold trophy that Pea had dropped. It had rolled into the gutter and now lay on its side, looking oddly bright and shiny when the day had turned so suddenly grey and miserable.

"Are you alright?" Toby asked, his voice quiet, afraid Pickle would snap back at him.

But when she turned to face him, her beautiful eyes were full of tears. "Is my auntie dead?" she asked.

Toby nodded. "I'm afraid so. I'm really sorry."

Pickle's breath hitched. "And ... and ... what about Candy?"

"There was only one hooman inside," Toby replied.

"Candy is *my* sister. Pickford's Incandescence. She and my auntie are inseparable."

Toby remembered the fluff on the grooming table. White poodle fluff.

"She's not there," he said.

Pickle lifted her head and howled.

CHAPTER SEVEN

"She might have run off," Pea suggested.

She was sitting on the tailgate of the ambulance, a blanket around her shoulders, tears rolling down her cheeks, supping a mug of strong tea that the café owner across the road had thoughtfully brought out for her. Clarissa had finished giving an initial statement to one of the detectives who'd turned up straight after the ambulance and had elected to stay with Pea for the time being.

"Yes, I suppose so," Clarissa said, but Toby knew this was a lie. The hatch had been closed and secured. Unless Candy had jumped over it—and logically this was a possibility too—then she had been removed from the premises through the back door.

Perhaps the detective was thinking the same thing. "There's a back entrance, isn't there? Did Hyacinth have a key?"

Hyacinth had been Pea's sister. Hyacinth and Peony.

Pea nodded. "Of course. We co-owned the business, although Cinth didn't do much in the way of dog grooming anymore. The key for the back door is on a hook at the rear of the shop behind the coat rack."

The detective made a note of that in her book. "Would she have entered through the front or the back?"

"The back. It's easier. There's an alarm system that's deactivated there."

"But the front door was open."

"We sometimes wedge it open on a hot day if the parlour has become a little stuffy or steamy. Just an inch or so. I imagine she did that. We use a door stopper. It's pink. I painted it. She thinks—thought—that was funny."

The detective gestured towards a sheet of A4 that had been pinned to the door apologising for the grooming salon's closure on Saturday afternoon. "So she wouldn't have kept the door locked once she was inside even though you were closed?"

Pea shrugged and sniffed. "I shouldn't have thought so. There's nothing of any value in there. Why would she have thought she was in any danger?" Pea began to sob again. Clarissa squeezed her shoulder.

"I appreciate these are difficult questions, Ms Shaw, but we're trying to build a picture."

"I know." Pea dashed a hand at her tears. "I'm fine."

"You're hardly fine," said Clarissa, "but that's okay. You're doing so well."

The detective agreed. "You are. Do you know why Hyacinth was on the premises today?"

"She texted me earlier asking if she could come in and use the facilities to give Candy a bath and trim. She could have done it at home ..." Pea pinched her nose, eyes firmly closed. "*Should* have done it at home! Then this would never have happened."

"What type of dog is Candy?"

"She's Pickle's sibling." Pea reached for Pickle, who nuzzled her hand. "A white poodle. Very similar to Pickle. Perhaps a little stockier."

"Do you know if anyone had a grudge against your sister? Did anyone wish her harm?"

Pea shook her head. "Not as far as I know."

"And *would* you have known?" the detective asked, arching an eyebrow, her tone delicate.

Pea seemed taken aback by this at first, but she reflected on the question before answering. "I think I would. We're close. Were close. I'm sure she'd tell me if she'd fallen out with someone ... would have told me." She drew in a shuddering breath. "Ugh. The past tense. I can't process ..."

"Do you have someone to stay with?" the detective asked, glancing at Clarissa. "You probably shouldn't be alone."

"I'll go to my brother's," Pea said, then slapped her thigh. "Oh no, I can't. He's not allowed dogs where he lives." She pointed up at the flat above the salon. "It'll be fine. I'll stay home."

"Unfortunately, that isn't a possibility," the detective said. "We're going to be conducting a thorough search of the premises."

"Oh!" Pea began to panic, her breathing ragged. "But I can't put Pickle in kennels!"

Toby had been listening closely to the entire conversation. Now his—Best in Show—eyebrows twitched and his ears fell flat. "Certainly not!" he said. "No-one deserves that!"

Clarissa nodded. "I don't know you very well, Pea," she said, "but I have a spare room and I'd be happy for you both to stay with us for as long as you need."

Fresh tears welled up in Pea's eyes. "That's so kind, but really, I couldn't."

"I understand," said Clarissa. "It is best to be with family at a time like this. The offer is there if you need it."

"We could take Pickle," Toby suggested.

Pickle's eyes widened and she started to pant. "I want to stay with Pea."

Clarissa evidently agreed with his idea, though. "What about if we looked after Pickle for you while you stay with your brother? Only until you were ready to return home, of course ..." she suggested.

Pea studied Pickle, her mouth turned down, her fingers twisted in the dog's collar among the rosettes.

"I'm sure it will only be a day or two," Clarissa said.

Without a word, Pea handed over Pickle's lead. "Th-th-thank you," she said.

"No!" Pickle clawed at Pea, who gently prised her off.

"Calm, baby. Be calm." She sniffled, leaned over and cradled Pickle's face.

"It's the least we can do." Clarissa spoke gently. "You have my mobile number. When you're ready, give me a shout and we'll return her to you. Or if you want to see her at any time, the same applies. She'll be well looked after, I promise."

"Properly pampered," Toby agreed, placing a paw on Pickle's shoulder. "We don't have much but what we do have is yours." A sudden thought occurred to him. "Except for my basket. That's mine." *Did that sound bad?* "During the daytime, it is. I suppose if *you* really wanted to, you could use it overnight. But just don't make it smell like a girl, okay?"

Hmmm. This wasn't coming out quite the way he wanted it to. "It's not that I have anything against girls, per se, it's just that when you smell of marshmallow and strawberry instead of rank rain puddle and three-day-old kebab, it's a little disconcerting."

Pickle stared at him, her eyes miserable.

"Also, I think in the interests of canine hygiene, we'd better not share food bowls. The water bowl is fine, and I can show you where the bird bath is at the back of Old Joe's garden."

Pickle's shoulders sagged.

Toby wagged his tail. "It's really nice. Full of rainwater. No fluoride."

"I just want to be with Pea."

Toby's chest squeezed. It wasn't that long since

his own heart had been broken. He would never get over losing Old Joe. Not ever. And he would never forgive The Pointy Woman.

Never, never, never.

"You can have my place on the sofa if you like?" he offered. "And I'll take you up to the roof of my wizard shack."

Pickle regarded him with slightly more interest. "Oh yes, you're a wizard. I forgot."

Toby wiggled his head, suddenly a little self-conscious. "In training."

"Well, if nothing else, I suppose this will be mildly entertaining," Pickle admitted, and pressed herself against Pea for one last hug.

CHAPTER EIGHT

Although subdued, Pickle soon settled in. Clarissa suggested she rest, and Toby again offered her his favourite spot in the sunshine but every time Clarissa moved, Pickle went with her. And of course, this meant that Toby had to go too, just in case he found himself missing out on something.

That would never do.

"Honestly, you two," Clarissa said, pouring herself a glass of water. "I feel like the Pied Piper of Hamelin. You don't have to accompany me everywhere. I'm not going anywhere!" She took her glass back into the living room and returned to her place behind her laptop. Pickle stuck to her heels, and

Clarissa relented and stroked her head. "Your fur is so beautifully soft," she said.

Toby huffed. "So's mine!" He tried to push in between Pickle and Clarissa but Clarissa held him at bay.

"Behave," she scolded. "And don't be jealous."

"I'm not jealous!" Toby lied.

"It's unbecoming," Clarissa reminded him and, one hand stroking Pickle's head, returned her attention to whatever she was reading onscreen.

Pickle smirked at Toby. "You're a green-eyed monster."

"My eyes are brown," Toby corrected her. "And I'm not jealous." He stalked off to his basket in front of the television and made a great show of roosting in it.

Pickle basked in Clarissa's attention a little longer but eventually, as always happened, Clarissa needed to type and withdrew her affection in favour of using both hands on her keyboard. Pickle remained where she was for a few minutes, considered lying on Clarissa's feet if only to ram the point home, but after glancing at Toby, she edged a little closer to him instead.

"You said I could have your basket," she reminded him.

"Overnight," Toby replied, his voice gruff, his face turned away.

Pickle tried again. "You said you'd show me your wizard shed."

"Wizard shack." This time Toby turned to look at her. "Sure, I can do that." He pushed himself up, glad to have something to do, but paused and narrowed his eyes. "You're not planning to jump into my basket as soon as I move, are you?"

Pickle pulled a face. "Ewww. No."

"Alright then." Toby relented and skipped past her. "Let's use my special exit!" He raced into the kitchen and jumped through the dog flap then, beaming, pivoted, ready to welcome Pickle into the back garden.

When she didn't immediately join him, he glared at the back door and muttered. "She's gone into my basket, hasn't she?"

He waited a few more seconds but impatience got the better of him. He poked his head through the flap, ready to call her name. The words jammed in his throat because, to his surprise, she was inches away from him, staring suspiciously at the door.

"What's the matter?" he asked.

Pickle backed away. "What is this trickery?"

"What? The flap?" Toby pushed his whole body

through and joined her. "It's a dog flap. It allows me to come and go at will."

"Without opening the door?" Pickle asked.

"That's right." Toby jumped back outside, did a half-turn and leapt through. The flap rattled and Pickle backed off a little further.

Sensing her discomfort, Toby put out a paw to stop the shimmy of the flap. "You don't have to go through so quickly," he said. "You can just step through. It's only that I get a little enthusiastic at times ..."

Clarissa's voice drifted through from the living room. "About most things."

Toby ignored her. "Watch," he told Pickle, and this time he pushed the flap with his nose and head and stepped through, one paw at a time. Once he was fully outside, he turned about and repeated the whole process. "See? It won't hurt you."

"I'm bigger than you," Pickle pointed out.

"A German shepherd can get through here. I know. We've tried—"

"You'd better not have!" came Clarissa's voice once more.

"Hahahaha!" Toby fake-laughed and jerked his head at Pickle. "Come on. Try it!"

Pickle took it slowly, just as Toby had done.

Nose. Head. Shoulders. One paw. Two paws. Body. Back paws. *Eureka!*

She arrived in the garden wagging her tail. "That's pure genius!" she said. "I'm going to ask Pea for one!"

Her face fell, remembering Pea, and Toby quickly took her mind off her owner by dashing back through into the kitchen and out again. "Try it faster!" he said.

Pickle, up for the challenge, went through a little more confidently. Then she bounced back into the garden. For the next few minutes, Toby and Pickle took turns trying to break the Guinness World Record for Speedy Dog-Flap Entrances and Exits until finally Clarissa could bear it no longer and bellowed at them. "Will you two just STOP!"

Giggling, Toby led Pickle over to his wizard shack. In actual fact, it had started life as a discarded shed, but Ed, Mr Sharpy, Conman and Clarissa had worked hard on turning the battered and decrepit structure into something entirely more solid. It had a door and a porthole and had been painted midnight blue and decorated with stars and planets. Up one side, a ladder-come-staircase led to a flat platform where Toby could either lie and watch the sky or commune with his cousins at the Twilight Barking.

The inside had started to take shape, too. The walls had been painted to match the exterior but without the stars, and the wooden floor had been covered in black linoleum. Shelves—a little wonky but endearingly so—graced one side of the shed, and Toby had begun to fill them with his treasures: books and stones and a beaten-up tennis ball and other odd items he'd collected on walks. Mrs Crouch had donated a red velvet curtain that ran along the entire back wall and lent the interior an air of mystery. A kind of tarot reader energy circa 1984. There were a couple of cushions on the floor, but so far no armchair—although this was high on Toby's want list—and no wood burner.

Clarissa insisted that a wood burner would be too dangerous in such an enclosed space, and besides which, she couldn't afford one.

Excuses, excuses, thought Toby.

His most recent acquisition had been a hand-painted sign gifted him by Mr Sharpy and his dog, Sparky, that read *Toby's Wizard Shack.*

And that was all that Toby needed to make it official.

"What do you think?" Toby asked Pickle as she stared up at the shed. Her face was giving nothing away.

"It's ... it's ... it's very *blue*."

Toby's brow creased.

"What's wrong with blue?"

Pickle shook her head. "We've had this conversation before."

"Although not to my satisfaction," Toby retorted.

"Not everything has to be about you," Pickle sniped.

"Ha!" Toby guffawed. "If you had your way, nothing would be about anyone except you!"

"Really, children." A soft voice from above halted the pair of sparring dogs in their tracks. They both lifted their heads to see Moriarty, the across-the-road neighbours' cat, staring down at them. "You're disturbing the peace."

"Are you friends with a *cat*?" Pickle asked Toby, her tone incredulous.

"Yes." Toby shrugged. "Why not?"

"He's friends with everyone," Moriarty told her. "He's a friendly chap."

"Cats and dogs are supposed to be mortal enemies," Pickle reminded him.

"I don't see why," Toby said. "Cats are creatures too. They deserve love, just as much as anyone else."

"Except mice," Moriarty suggested.

"*Even* mice!" Toby disagreed. "*And* birds."

"You're just no fun, sometimes," Moriarty said. She stared at Pickle long and hard. "Is it safe for me to come down or is this one going to eat me?"

"She's not going to eat you," Toby promised. "Come on down. I have some treats in the shack."

Moriarty narrowed her eyes at Pickle, who shuffled uncomfortably and then backed away.

"Sure," she said. "I won't eat you."

Moriarty took the staircase part of the way, then finished with a graceful leap. Once all four paws were on the ground, she asked, "Did you mention treats?"

"Come on in." Toby led the pair of them inside the shed. Moriarty politely waited until Pickle had settled on the biggest cushion before taking her place by the door, neatly curling her tail around herself.

Toby had an old Quality Street tin that Mrs Crouch had given him. Every few days she replenished it with an assortment of treats. Ostensibly they were 'dog' treats, but she'd let on that cats could eat them too. This was fortunate because Moriarty had become a frequent visitor.

Although dogs, lacking as they do opposable thumbs, would generally struggle to open anything, Toby had mastered the art of magickally lifting the lid. He would then distribute the treats through a levitation spell. The treats, sometimes cheese, sometimes tuna or salmon, occasionally ham or bacon —*NOM!*—would soar through the air where the waiting recipient could snatch at them and chomp them on the go or, more politely, allow the treats to settle into a small pile to the side so they could be savoured.

It all rather depended on who was visiting Toby. Pippin and Troot were big snatchers, but Sparky and Moriarty were picky and liked to guard their treats for a while before nibbling gently.

It turned out that Pickle was more of the latter type of guest, but she seemed quite taken with the way Toby could move things through the air.

Moriarty levelled her cool, green gaze on Pickle. "What brings you to our neighbourhood?" she asked.

Pickle, instantly plunged into the trauma she'd endured earlier, began to pant.

"It's okay," said Toby. "I'll explain." He cocked his head to one side. "If you don't mind?"

"You might as well," Moriarty told him. "Twilight Barking isn't far away, and no doubt there'll be lots of gossip about anything that may be amiss ..."

Toby had a feeling she might already have heard something over the Catvine, but anyway, she had a point. They were on the cusp of autumn and the light was beginning to fade earlier. There would be plenty of chat in a few minutes.

"Pickle here is staying with us for a day or two," Toby told Moriarty, who closed her eyes and concentrated on what he was saying. The first time she'd done this, Toby had assumed she'd fallen asleep, but apparently this was the way that Moriarty preferred to take in information. She would relax, close her eyes and think intelligent thoughts. Well, that's what she said, anyway.

"Her hooman is Pea, or Peony, who runs a poodle parlour in Mayflower Lane. I visited there earlier this week," he reminded Moriarty, in case she'd forgotten.

Moriarty's eyebrows twitched.

"Earlier today, myself—intrepid hound of magick and mystery—and Clarissa—roving reporter of paranormal wrongdoings—stumbled across a body in said poodle parlour."

Pickle cried softly.

"At first, Clarissa—roving reporter—"

"Get on with it," muttered Moriarty.

Toby pouted. "Okay! Keep your fur on! I was trying to make it exciting!"

"It was probably exciting enough to begin with," Moriarty pointed out.

Pickle made a small noise in her throat.

Instantly contrite, Toby bowed his head. "Sorry," he said.

"Continue," Moriarty ordered.

"Clarissa thought the body we found belonged to Pea, Pickle's owner, but it turned out to be Pea's sister."

"Does her name begin with a *p* too?" Moriarty asked. "Because there's a lot of *p*s going on."

"No," said Pickle. "She's called Hyacinth. Cinth for short. She was lovely."

"I'm sorry for your loss," said Moriarty, then nodded at Toby. "Continue."

"Hyacinth—Cinth, if I may—had been using the salon to groom her own dog, Pickle's sister—"

"Candy," said Pickle.

"Goodness me, I think I need to draw a family tree," Moriarty said.

"To cut a long story short," said Toby, "Candy is now missing, and Cinth had a pair of grooming scissors stuck in her neck."

"Oh dear." Moriarty opened her eyes. "So ... whodunnit?"

Pickle regarded her with surprise. "If we knew that, I'd be safe at home with Pea and the killer would have been arrested and ... and ..." She sniffled. "But it wouldn't bring Cinth and Candy back."

"Candy may well come back yet," Toby reminded her. "There is a chance that she ran off because she was scared."

"I am surprised that you haven't solved the mystery yet," Moriarty told Toby.

"I'm not sure solving hooman murders is quite my speciality," Toby protested.

"But you did it once before," Moriarty reminded him.

Pickle's ears perked up. "Did you?"

Toby wobbled his head. "Ye-es." He sighed. "But I didn't bring The Pointy Woman to justice."

"You will," Moriarty said, sounding sure of herself.

"I appreciate your confidence in my abilities," Toby said. "But—"

"Have you ever solved a missing person's case?" Pickle asked.

Toby thought back to Grace Catesby, Clarissa's old schoolteacher. He'd solved that, hadn't he? He nodded.

"Excellent," said Pickle. "Then I want you to find Candy for me."

"Find Candy," Toby repeated, recalling the crime scene and, more importantly, the lack of clues.

Outside, the sky had turned pale peach at the horizon, darker blue higher up. From down the road came the excited bark of Vita the Labrador.

The Twilight Barking had started.

"No time like the present," said Moriarty, and the three of them made their way out of the shed and up the stairs onto the platform.

CHAPTER NINE

"Nobody knows anything," Pickle lamented.

They'd remained on the platform for nearly an hour until the stars had come out and the neighbourhood had fallen completely silent. Finally, Clarissa had called them in for dinner.

"Nobody knows anything *yet*," Toby said, chewing on something from his bowl that was supposed to be rabbit. "You said yourself that this was your first Twilight Barking. Keep that in mind. In my experience, you have to allow these things to trickle down. Not everyone—like yourself—can get to a Twilight Barking, so they catch up via word of mouth or through gossiping with other dogs they meet while they're out and about."

"But the trail will get cold," said Pickle.

"It will become cooler but not cold," said Toby. "*Never* cold. Trust me."

Pickle picked at her dinner.

Toby, who'd finished his in thirty seconds flat, eyed her temporary bowl with longing. "If you don't want that, I'd be more than happy to help you out," he said.

Pickle stood back. "Help yourself." She watched him polish off her biscuits in record time.

"Better not tell Clarissa," he said, licking his lips.

"Tell me what?" Clarissa asked, coming into the kitchen with her plate and cutlery. She'd been eating in front of the television—which she always claimed was not great for her digestion, but she did it anyway.

"That I said we'd help Pickle search for Candy," Toby said, then pretended to realise what he was saying. "Oops."

"You don't fool me, buddy. You've eaten Pickle's dinner!"

"I didn't eat all of it," Toby protested. "Just the leftover biscuits. The bits she didn't want."

Clarissa reached down to stroke Pickle. "Did you have enough to eat? He didn't bully you, did he?"

Pickle surprised Toby then. "No," she said. "He's been a gentleman."

"Steady," said Toby. "I have a reputation to maintain."

"What did she say?" Clarissa asked, glancing between the two.

Toby preened. "That I've been a gentleman."

"Pffft!" Clarissa giggled. "Alright, as long as you're sure." She left the dogs to it and began to run the hot tap into the bowl in the sink.

Pickle watched her do so. "Reminds me of home," she said. "Clearing up after dinner. I hope Pea's alright."

"These things take time," Toby told her. "She needs to work through the shock and denial and the anger, and eventually, sometime in the future, with your help, she'll come to a place of acceptance."

"You're really quite wise for a mongrel," observed Pickle and traipsed through to the living room.

Toby followed her and grabbed hold of the remote before jumping onto the couch. Pickle stood in the centre of the room, unsure where to settle. "Come on up here," said Toby, scootching across. "What do you fancy watching? David Attenborough? A baking show? Oooh! I know!" His paw hovering over the remote, he scanned through the channels until he found what he was looking for. "*Midsomer Murders*! I love this!"

They lay side by side, snouts hanging over the edge of the couch, watching the action unfold. Clarissa came out to join them and squidged in beside them, folding one leg under herself. "We've seen this," she tried to say, but neither dog reacted and there was no way Toby was going to surrender the remote control, so she was forced to watch with them until the credits rolled at ten o'clock.

Clarissa yawned and stretched. "Do you two want to walk around the block or are you happy enough to go in the garden?" she asked.

"I think we'll stay in the garden," Toby said. It had been a long day, with a lot of walking around. In fact, he may well have been resting his eyes during part of the programme.

"Good." Clarissa pulled herself up. "I'll go up. I'll see you in a bit. Pickle, you're welcome to sleep anywhere you like."

"I'll make sure to show her some good spots," Toby told her, wagging his tail.

Both dogs attended to business quickly enough in the garden, but Pickle seemed loathe to go back inside. Toby stopped at the door. "It's bedtime," he reminded her.

"I know ..." Pickle tipped her head up to look at the stars. In return, they solemnly blinked at her, the wide, infinite skies reinforcing the magnitude of her loss. "Do you think Pea is thinking of me?"

"I'm sure she is," said Toby. "And Candy too."

"I hope she's alright." Pickle drew closer to Toby. "Thank you for agreeing to help me. Do you think we'll find her?"

"I may not be Inspector Barnaby, but I have a few tricks up my sleeve," said Toby. "Not that I wear sleeves, but you know what I mean."

"If only we could find some witnesses," said Pickle. In the episode of *Midsomer Murders* they'd been watching John Nettles had benefitted enormously from several witness accounts.

"You never know. The Twilight Barking might provide a lead—" Toby stopped.

"What is it?" Pickle asked. "What have you thought of?"

"Witnesses," said Toby. "Why didn't I think of it before? There may well have been witnesses to Hyacinth's murder."

"Who?" Pickled demanded. "We'll have to talk to them!"

"Hold your horses there, pardner," said Toby, affecting the worst Texan accent a dog ever had the cheek to muster. "When I went into the parlour this afternoon, I spotted something over in the corner near the back door where the floorboards don't meet the skirting board properly. Are there mice living in the shop?"

"Mice?" Pickle curled her lip. "I don't think so ..."

"Hmm." Toby's face fell. "I thought I saw whiskers, that's all."

"Whiskers?" Pickle nodded. "Yes, you probably did. There are some rats living beneath the floorboards. Pea has considered having an exterminator out, but she loves animals too much and didn't relish the idea of having a load of rat corpses below her feet."

"Rats?" Toby's eyes lit up. "Even better than mice." He pondered for a few seconds. "You know? Why shouldn't we go and have a conversation with them?"

"Now?" Pickle glanced around as though it wasn't obvious to Toby that it was nighttime.

"You wanted witnesses, and now we've found some, so let's make hay while the erm ... moon shines."

CHAPTER TEN

While Toby felt quite at home roaming the streets of Sun Valley by himself, even at night, this was a totally new experience for Pickle. She'd only ever been out and about with Pea, and even when she was allowed off lead, she always stayed close by because that's how she'd been trained. It had never occurred to her to go off-piste, to coin a phrase.

The only drawback with being out and about after dark, from Toby's point of view, was that people were much more likely to imagine you were a stray. On the plus side, most hoomans couldn't be bothered to report a stray dog to the council once the offices were closed, so they tended not to approach or get involved. In addition, strays weren't generally considered a police matter, so whenever he did venture out, he remained largely untroubled. But there was always the off chance some do-gooder, or someone with a little too much alcoholic joie de vivre, would try and catch them.

Happily for Toby, the pair of them made it into town without exciting too much attention—with the forgettable exception of a couple of partygoers outside a pub who wanted a cuddle—and paused to huddle in the shadows at the top of Mayflower Lane, staring down towards the marketplace. The muted streetlights clearly showed the tape cordon that remained in situ outside Sweet Pea's Parlour for Pampered Pooches. The few pedestrians around, mainly young people probably heading towards the nightclubs on King Street, gave the area a wide berth.

"Perhaps we should have waited until morning," suggested Pickle. "Everything looks more sinister in the dark."

"There's nothing to be scared of," Toby assured her. "You stay here a second. I want to run down and look inside."

"You're going to break in?" Pickle whispered.

"No, not now. Not here. My concern is being seen when I do so, which is more likely at the front. I just want to look through the window." Toby scampered along the lane, his claws making soft tippy-tapping sounds on the road. Being short, he didn't have to duck under the tape, but he did have to plant his front paws on the window ledge to haul himself upright so he could see inside.

The lights were off.

There was nothing to see and no-one inside. *Good, good*, thought Toby. All four paws back on the ground, he took a few steps and examined the front door. It had been locked and seals attached. He'd imagined this would be the case, hence the reason he'd prefer to enter through the back door.

"Let's do it," he whispered to himself, and scampered back to where Pickle was waiting.

"What did you see?" Pickle asked, sounding anxious.

"There's nothing *to* see. It's all dark and closed up."

"Do you think we'd be better off going through the back?" Pickle asked. "Pea and I use the back door all the time."

"Absolutely."

"Follow me."

They doubled back on themselves and trotted a little way along the pavement that ran parallel to the park before Pickle indicated a narrow inlet that Toby had never spotted before. It ran between a gift shop and a phone shop and was only wide enough for two people to pass. A quick right turn along the rear of the gift shop, then a left and they found themselves in an alleyway. To their right were the yards belonging to the Mayflower Lane properties. Some of these were open to the alley, some of them walled with gates.

Halfway down was the rear of Peony's salon.

"This is it." Pickle stood on her back legs and pushed the gate. It squealed as it opened. "The lock on this has been busted since Pea took over. She keeps saying she'll replace the whole gate, but she never does."

"Lucky for us," said Toby. "And probably the murderer."

Pickle shuddered.

They climbed the few steps up to the back door. There could be no mistaking they were in the right place. This side of the door was as pink as the rest of Pea's parlour.

Toby lifted his paw, preparing to utter a few words and open the door, but Pickle stopped him. "Wait!"

"What?" Alarmed, Toby spun around, expecting someone to be coming for them.

"What if Hu-hu-Hyacinth is still inside?"

Toby hadn't thought of this. "That's unlikely, isn't it?" he asked, more to reassure himself than Pickle. "I mean, I don't think the police would leave a corpse alone in situ, would they? There would be someone here."

The dogs looked at each other. Pickle said nothing, unwilling to commit. "I don't think they would," decided Toby. "What if someone came in and ... and tampered with the body? The body is evidence!" Toby knew this from watching countless episodes of his favourite detective shows.

"Alright," said Pickle. "If you think so."

Toby nodded. He tipped back and went up on his hind legs, just about tall enough to touch the lock with a front paw. He waved it over the old-fashioned keyhole. "*Aperta*!"

"Wait!" Pickle hissed.

The lock clicked.

Toby glanced across at Pickle. "What?"

"The alarm system. There's a loud clanging thing if you set it off. It'll wake up the whole town!"

"Oh. Do you know the code?"

"I don't."

"Useful." Toby scanned his memory for alarm deactivation spells. He couldn't come up with one, but he could possibly combine a 'shush' spell with an 'obliterate' spell if push came to shove. "Let's see what happens."

Another wave of his paw and the handle turned. He pressed against the door until it was slightly ajar and tipped forward onto his front feet. Holding his breath, he listened.

No alarm.

"The police can't have reactivated it," Toby surmised. "Probably for ease of getting in and out."

"Maybe Pea forgot to give them the code," Pickle said.

Toby nodded. He peered into the murky parlour, ears straining for the slightest scratch of a rat.

Of course, he and Pickle had been conversing and the door had made a noise, so any rats in the immediate vicinity would know they were coming. He couldn't hear them, but that didn't mean they weren't there.

Toby took a few tentative steps inside. The parlour smelled different now, somehow. Whereas previously the overwhelming scent had been fruity-flavoured shampoo, now there were more metallic smells. And chemicals. Not particularly pleasant. He poked his head around the door. The body was gone but the puddle of dark blood—made darker by the lack of light—remained in place. Yellow markers were scattered around too, each numbered by a crime scene officer and luminescing in the limited light available.

"We'll have to tread carefully," Toby whispered to Pickle over his shoulder, "otherwise the police will know we've been in here."

"Maybe it would be better if I stayed outside?" Pickle ventured. "Kept watch or something?"

"I need your help to speak with the rats," Toby said, backing out of the salon. Pickle was shaking, he noticed. "It will be fine, I promise. Hyacinth isn't here anymore."

"Wh-what if her ghost is in there?"

"If her ghost is there, she'll be able to tell us who killed her and where Candy is," Toby couldn't help pointing out. "But trust me. There's no ghost."

"Al-al-alright."

Toby slipped through the door once more. Out of respect for Pickle and her loss, he moved away to allow her room so she could see the whole salon without being crammed in the corner by the door. She came in, her ears drooping, quickly surveyed the scene, then dropped her head as if in quiet contemplation. Toby followed suit, paying his respects to a woman he hadn't known but who'd evidently meant the world to her loved ones.

When Pickle was done, she took a deep breath. "Let's find Candy," she said, and turned to the gap in the floorboards. Toby joined her. Together they sniffed at the hole. All was quiet, but Toby had a definite sense that the rats were close by. He pondered on the best way to proceed. In his experience, the key that opened even the most recalcitrant of doors tended to be politeness.

Or magick.

But he opted to try politeness first.

"Excuse me there, sirs?" he called.

Not so much as a rustle.

"They may not be 'sirs'," Pickle quietly pointed out.

"True," agreed Toby. He tried again. "Excuse me there, sirs and madams?"

Nothing.

"We know you're in there," Pickle snarled. "You might—"

Toby nudged her out of the way. "Softly, softly," he said. Pickle sighed and Toby started again. "Excuse me, *good* sirs and madams. My name is Toby and I'm a spellbound hound. I'm with Pickle—"

"Pickford's Afterglow," Pickle reminded him.

"—who actually resides on these premises—"

"Upstairs," Pickle inserted. "They probably haven't been there!" she said when Toby widened his eyes at her.

"Babe." A male voice—with a definite cockney twang—rasped from somewhere beyond the skirting board. "If you think we 'aven't been everywhere in this building, you must 'ave been born yesterday."

"This morning, more like," said another male voice, this one as soft and as whispery as sugar paper.

"Huyeh, huyeh, huyeh!" The pair of them snickered away together.

Pickle crinkled her nose. "Ewww."

Toby doubled down on his polite approach. "I hope you've found yourself most welcome wherever you visit."

"Whatever," came the first voice, deep and husky.

"We were wondering whether you'd be able to assist us," Toby said, his snout so close to the hole, he could have slipped his nose inside.

"Nah, mate," the first rat said.

"I knew it," grumbled Pickle.

But Toby wasn't one to give up so easily. "We're not here to harm you. You have my word."

"A dog's word ain't worth the breath it's spoken with," said the first rat.

"What we're after is some information—"

"We don't know nuffink. Nuffink at all."

Pickle growled in exasperation. "Seriously, Toby. This is a waste of time! Since when did a rat ever help anyone except themselves? They have no honour!"

"S'nice, innit?" the first rat asked. "You don't know nuffink abaaaht us! And there you is, running our names down!"

"We're community-minded fellows," the second rat protested. "We look after each other!"

"Isn't that my point?" Pickle grouched. "You look after each other but you don't look out for anyone else!"

"'Ere!"

Pickle was on a roll. "Because if you did, you'd help us find the person who murdered my auntie!"

"Ooh!" The second rat's breath exploded out of him. "Look. See. Did she say murder?"

"She did say murder," the first rat replied.

"That would've been all that commotion earlier on, wouldn't it?"

Toby pounced—on the rat's words, not the rat himself. "So you did hear something, after all!"

"We didn't say we didn't hear nuffink," said the first rat. "We said we didn't know nuffink. That's a massive difference."

Pickle tipped her head back and groaned.

Toby, however, continued practising patience. "We'd be terribly grateful if you'd share what you heard."

A pair of whiskers appeared at the hole. "How grateful?" The soft voice of the second rat.

From behind him the first rat asked, "Yeah. How grateful is terribly grateful?"

"Define gratefulness, please," the second rat requested, his black beady eye appearing at the hole.

"How grateful would you like me to be?" Toby asked. "I mean, what would gratefulness look like to you if I was to be grateful for you spilling the beans about all you may have seen and heard this afternoon?"

The whiskers and the eye disappeared. There followed a hushed conversation and a few squeaks. Toby and Pickle exchanged glances. Toby shrugged. Eventually, new whiskers appeared at the entrance to the hole. The first rat.

"A kweesh."

"A what?" Toby frowned. "What's a kweesh?"

"What's a kweesh?" the rat repeated. "What's a

kweesh? It's a big cheese pie without a top. Some of 'em has bacon in which makes 'em even lovelier in my opinion. Mate, you ain't lived if you ain't eaten kweesh!"

"He means quiche," said Pickle, whose picnics tended to be upmarket.

"Of course. Quiche," Toby nodded.

"Quiche. Kweesh. Whatever. We wants a whole one of them."

A whole quiche? "Right." Toby wracked his brains. Where was he likely to acquire a quiche from in the middle of the night?

"And that's not all." The first rat was warming to his theme. "We wants some 'Ob-k-nobs."

This was easier to decipher despite the rat pronouncing the otherwise silent *k*. Clarissa was partial to Hobnobs of the dark chocolate variety, although she'd never share with Toby because he wasn't allowed chocolate.

"Hobnobs, okay," said Toby.

"A whole packet of aforementioned delectables. No skimpin' mate, no skimpin'."

"Anything else?" Toby asked.

"Cheese," said the first rat. "We're totes partial to a bit of cheese."

Toby could identify. "Who isn't?"

"Is that everything?" Pickle asked.

"It's a downpayment, for sure," said the first rat.

The second rat laughed. "Huyeh, huyeh, huyeh!"

"Alright," Toby agreed. There's always a price for information. Some sort of exchange to be made. A favour here, a favour there. "We'll go and see what we can find." He edged away. "We'll be back soon."

As soon as he'd vacated his spot beside the hole, Pickle dived straight in there. "You'd better tell us what we want to know," she snapped. "A deal is a deal, and I for one don't want to be messing around with you guys."

"Hey!" the first rat cried in an injured tone. "Getouttahere!"

Toby pulled Pickle away. "We *are* getting out of here! We're off to find you your ... delectables. We won't be long."

"Yeah?" The rat sounded as though he were dusting himself off. "Take the psycho lady away and transplant her with a better attitude. We're serious businessmen 'ere!"

"Serious!" agreed the second rat. "Seriously serious!"

"No problem," said Toby. "Glad to hear it. Otherwise, we might have to get serious too!"

"You and whose army?" the first rat asked. "Trust me, fur kid. You don't wanna mess with the Mayflower Lane Mafia."

"The what now?" Toby glanced at Pickle, hoping she'd be able to shed some light, but she only looked blankly back at him.

"The Mayflower Lane Mafia, mate. We're five thousand strong!"

"Five thousand *rats*?" Pickle shuddered.

"And growing every day!" the second rat added.

"Every second of every day," the first rat muttered. "Babies here, babies there."

"Can't escape," the second rat added, sounding forlorn.

"Yeah, it's a baby boom alright. Hardly any room to move in the sewers." The first rat raised his voice again for the benefit of Pickle and Toby. "So don't you be coming back 'ere shouting the odds about how you're gonna be getting serious, cos trust me, fella, we can get seriouser."

That's not even a word, thought Toby.

"Seriously seriouser," said the second rat.

"Alright," said Toby. "We'll be back soon." He nodded at Pickle. "Let's go."

He led Pickle out the back door and down the

few steps. They didn't bother shutting the door. Toby didn't intend for them to take too long.

"Where are we going?" Pickle asked. "How are we going to get those items?"

"Unfortunately, I'm not sure we have much choice. We'll go to Clarissa's favourite mini-market and"—he grimaced—"we're going to have to steal them."

CHAPTER ELEVEN

"Are you clear what you're doing?" Toby asked Pickle.

They were huddling beside the bicycle rack outside the mini-market, trying to stay out of the way of the few customers going in or coming out.

"I go up to the counter and do my best pleading face—"

"Eyes and teeth, eyes and teeth," Toby reminded her.

"Yes, a big goofy smile—" Pickle broke off. "You know, this is so demeaning. A dog with my talents. A *show* dog with my talents!"

"Listen, if I ever need anyone to do a *Dogue* centrespread, I'll come to you, okay?" Toby said.

"As long as it's not *Playdog*. I am *so* not that kind

of girl." Pickle minced around, turning her head to the left and then the right, pouting or staring down her elegant snout, pretending to pose for the paparazzi.

"Focus!" Toby implored Pickle. "I need you to keep the cashier distracted long enough for me to find all three items and bring them outside. Then, somehow, we have to carry three things back to the salon between us."

"We only have two mouths," said Pickle.

"That's my point," said Toby. He had started to doubt Pickle's intelligence. He sighed. "Can you do this, do you think?"

Pickle tossed her head. "Of course I can!"

"Good. Are you ready?"

"Baby, I was born ready," Pickle said and sashayed up to the door. It opened automatically and she disappeared inside. Toby waited until it opened again—a customer exiting the store with a four-pack of cider and an enormous packet of crisps—then dashed inside and straight up the first aisle.

He'd never ventured inside the store before—Clarissa always made him wait outside—but he was immediately taken by how clean and shiny everything was and what a riot of colour and range of scents bombarded his senses. The overwhelming whiffs were of soap powder and detergents, but the fruit and vegetables were properly pungent too. A radio was playing some sort of bhangra music. Toby bopped his head along with it for a moment—how could you fail not to—but quickly remembered he was on a mission and needed to be deadly serious.

"Cheese, biscuits ... and what was it?" *Ugh!* Momentarily, Toby had forgotten the third item. His gaze fell on the chiller at the top of the aisle. "Kweesh!" he muttered. "Kweesh! How could I forget."

He made his way to the end of the aisle and stood where the shelves blocked him from the direct eyeline of the cashier.

"Hello, gorgeous," a young Asian man on the till was saying. "Where's your owner?"

"We don't call them owners," Pickle told him, not that he'd be able to understand what she was saying. "We own ourselves, thank you very much."

Don't get too snarky, thought Toby. *Eyes and teeth, eyes and teeth.*

"Did they come in with you? Because we don't allow dogs inside—" the young man continued.

Uh-oh. This could spell trouble. What if he came out from behind the counter and began looking for Pickle's owner? He'd spot Toby and then they'd both be turfed out. Toby recognised he needed to hurry, and he needed Pickle to pull something out of the bag.

She began to sing.

Woo-oooo-woooooo woo-oooo-ooooo!

It was terrible.

Woo-ooo-oooooooo-ooooo-oooooooow!

Really bad.

But the cashier began to laugh. "Do you like this music?" he asked and turned it up.

Wooo-ooo-ooo-ooo-ooo!

Good one, Pickle! Now where's the kweesh? Toby stood back on his rear legs to make himself taller, scanning the shelves for something that looked like a lidless cheese pie. *Coleslaw. Cheese dip. Ooh, yummy. Clotted cream. Cheese. Pasty. Wait! Cheese!*

That was one of the things on the list. Quick as a flash, Toby reached for the largest packet he could find and snapped at it. He secured it, but not without several of the cheeses behind it choosing to jump off the shelf and smack onto the tiled floor. Toby held his breath, but perhaps the music was too loud because the young man didn't leave his place at the counter.

Toby sprinted along the aisle. His luck was in. As he reached the entrance, someone else came in and he was able to dive outside without being noticed. *Perfect timing*, he thought, and deposited the packet of cheese next to the bicycle rack where it wasn't immediately obvious.

Taking up a position next to the automatic door, he waited for the customer to grab the few things he wanted—it looked like some chocolate and a big bag of disposable nappies. Toby, staying low and hiding off to the side, peeped around the corner. The customer and the cashier were laughing at Pickle, who was both singing—if you could call it that—and dancing.

Doggy dancing. Bottom twerking, shaking and shimmying while stamping her paws in time to the energetic bhangra beat. Finally, as the customer grinned, waved at the cashier and made his way out, Toby sneaked in. He almost forgot about taking cover down the aisle, so entranced was he by Pickle's performance, but time was of the essence.

Back at the chiller, he realised that the kweeshes were on the very bottom shelf, along with some pizzas. Trying not to be distracted by chicken and bacon pizza, Toby scanned the flavours available. *Spinach and blue cheese? Ugh. Cheese and onion. A little plain, although the rats might like it because of the cheese content.* However, on balance, Toby decided the little fellows would prefer a proper Quiche Lorraine.

Doghandling the cardboard package was easier thought than done. The items at the bottom of the chiller were in some kind of tray and, without opposable thumbs, lifting them out was tricky.

Unless you were a spellbound hound who could perform levitation spells, that is.

Why didn't I think of this before? Toby wondered. *Of course I can carry more than one item.*

He parked moving the Quiche Lorraine for a moment and dodged along the top of the aisles, searching for the one most likely to have the biscuit display. He knew the mini-market kept Hobnobs because Clarissa frequently bought them from here.

There they are!

Toby recognised the packaging. *Dark chocolate? Milk chocolate? Plain?*

They do plain Hobnobs? Why has Clarissa never told me this? Hmm.

But he knew very well why. If she had to admit that they made plain Hobnobs, he'd have insisted she buy some for him.

Cunning, thought Toby, and levitated a packet of milk chocolate Hobnobs off the shelf.

To return to the chiller, he now had to pass the

crisps section. The bright yellow packaging of the Quavers—the most delicious cheesy, starchy, rice-flour snack of all time—caught his eye. Almost without thinking, he levitated a 'family-sized'—hungry Toby-sized, in fact—bag from the shelf and made his way back to the chiller.

His levitation skills had been coming on in leaps and bounds, but he had been mainly practising the ability to lift and hold heavier items; he hadn't really considered the logistics of holding a number of objects at once. Nevertheless, after a couple of false starts—most notably the packet of biscuits hitting the floor—Toby managed to juggle all three items.

Now all he had to do was get out.

The music stopped.

Oops.

Toby froze, frightened of making any kind of noise. His shopping hung in the air behind him.

"You're so funny," the young man said. "But you have to go. My brother's going to be down in a minute 'cos we'll be closing up soon. And he doesn't like dogs. Where's your owner?"

"Who knows," said Pickle. "And in fact, it's probably better for everyone involved that she doesn't know what I'm currently getting up to. My partner-in-crime is robbing you blind, and you're too daft to notice."

Harsh, thought Toby.

"Are you ready yet, Toby?" Pickle complained. "Our man here is getting angsty!"

"Hush, now," said the cashier. "Out you go." Toby heard the click of the little door that separated the cashier and the tills from the shop proper. If the cashier came out and shepherded Pickle to the door, he would see Toby in the middle of the aisle balancing his goodies.

Toby hurriedly glanced around, looking for something to distract the cashier. He noted the bottles behind the tills—not wines, but the more expensive spirits. Uttering a prayer for forgiveness, he reached out with his mind and tried to knock one from the shelf.

Unfortunately, he was already juggling three items, and he simply didn't have the skill to manage another one. Rather like tapping your head and rubbing your stomach, Toby couldn't hold up three items and let one fall. The second he envisaged the bottle falling, the quiche, the biscuits and the mega packet of Quavers tumbled to the floor.

"What was that?" the cashier asked.

"Run, Pickle!" Toby barked, then quickly levitating his three items and leaving the bottle on the shelf to live another day, he bounded for the door. Fortunately, Pickle reached it first, activating the sensor that caused it to open. Both dogs sprinted through and swerved hard right, the shopping keeping pace. Behind them the cashier was shouting, but he didn't chase after them. They kept going until they found the inlet next to the gift shop and dived into the alley.

Panting, they waited, ears pricked. Would the cashier come after them? Would he send his brother or, even worse, the police?

Pickle giggled softly. "Boy, that was such fun!"

"Don't get used to it," said Toby, who had a feeling that parts of his fur were now even greyer than they were before.

Pickle, still tittering, looked up at the goods hovering above their heads.

"What's in the yellow bag?"

"Crisps," said Toby. "Quavers. I just had a bit of a craving for them."

"But where's the cheese?" she asked.

"Oh, bum!" Toby tutted. "I left it by the bike rack."

"What?" Pickle poked her head around the corner of the gift shop, peering back towards the mini-market, several streetlights illuminating the way. "You'll have to go and grab it," she said.

"Why can't you go?"

"He's more likely to recognise me than you."

"I suppose so," Toby grumbled. He began to walk off.

"Wait!" Pickled called him back. "Are you seriously going to walk back out there in public with things hanging in the air above you?"

Toby tipped his head back. He reasoned it would look odd to the casual observer. He gently placed the items on the ground.

"You guard these," he said, "while I go back."

"Will do," Pickle agreed.

"And don't eat any!"

"As if I would."

"You're a dog. Of course you would. We need to get this lot to the rats, and I don't want to have to go through that whole rigmarole again."

"I wouldn't mind." Pickle shrugged. "Maybe we could start a heist gang? Rob a few other convenience stores."

Toby groaned. "Let's not, okay? It's wrong to steal. I wouldn't be doing this at all unless I was desperate."

"Yeah." Pickle poked at the Quavers. "Because these just accidentally followed you."

Point taken.

"Keep your paws off them," Toby said, and exited in pursuit of a cheese.

CHAPTER TWELVE

"Hello?" All was quiet back in the salon, and Toby was afraid the rats had done a runner while he and Pickle had been out. "Hello? Hey, guys?"

"Whaddayawant?" A pair of whiskers appeared at the hole, but this time the voice had a strong New York accent.

"Oh, er, hi," said Toby. "We come bearing gifts."

"We likes gifts," the rat said. "But it ain't my birthday, so what gives?"

"Are the erm ... the fellows I was talking to earlier around?" Toby asked.

"Ya got names?" the American rat asked. "Only there's an army of us down here."

"I didn't get any names, no," said Toby.

Pickle nudged him out of the way and drew closer to the hole. "Hey! Rat features!" she bellowed. "We're doing business here, so fetch the two idiots we were talking to before or I'll start searching the cupboards for some rat poison!"

"No need to be so goddamn rude!" the rat shouted back.

Pickle backed away and sniffed at one of Pea's cupboards. "I'm sure Pea stores it in here."

"A'right! A'right. Keep your everloving dog hair on!" The whiskers disappeared from the hole. "Yo!" the American rat called. "Yo, Sal? Pom? Come on up here!"

The first rat's voice came from a distance away. "I'm on a break!"

"Gedduphere! You're never on a break from being a member of the Mayflower Lane Mafia. Besides. We've got ourselves a situation here."

"What what what?" the first rat grumbled, coming closer.

"You been having dealings with some dogs, Sal?" the American rat asked, and there was something in his voice that sent a chill along even Toby's spine.

"Not on purpose, Persil, I swear." The first rat, Sal, had turned into a grovelling wretch.

"That ain't what it looks like from here. What's

that pair of rabid stinkhounds doing outside my hole?"

"Aw, come on, Persil," Sal whined. "It's a poodle parlour. There's always dogs in there. The white one with the fluff, especially."

"They said they come bearing gifts," said Persil. "I likes gifts."

"Oh, sure, sure. The gifts are for you, Persil."

There was a slapping sound. The first rat squawked. "You blowing smoke up my ass, Sal? Cos no-one does that to Persil Sollozzo. Not if they want to see the dawning of another day."

"No, Persil, I promise!" rasped the first rat. *Sal?* Toby reminded himself, trying to keep track of the names.

"They're here for information," the papery voice of the second rat confessed. "There was an incident this afternoon. Yesterday afternoon, now."

"I see," Persil said. "Well, you know, any visitors have to go through the main man first."

"Of course, of course. It was never our intention to take the gifts for ourselves ..." Sal whimpered.

Persil snorted. "Rancid liars. You're not even very good at that."

"Excuse me?" Toby called politely. "Would anybody like these ... delectables?"

Persil's whiskers twitched at the hole in the skirting boards, scenting out the goodies. "They have to be passed over to Don Goryonli," he said.

"How do I meet Don?" asked Toby, beginning to think he was losing the war here. Were these rats going to pass him around from pillar to post and never reach an endpoint? This was all rather exhausting. He should have been tucked up at home on Old Joe's old bed, Clarissa snoring in the room next door.

"His name's not Don, he *is* a don!" Persil corrected him. "A rat mafia don!"

"One of the best," said Sal, reaching peak obsequiousness.

"*The* best," said Persil.

"The *very* best," said Sal.

A mafia don? This news gave Toby pause. What kind of trouble could a member of the rat mafia cause? Did he want this on his doorstep? Not really.

He was about to abandon this whole sorry situation when Pickle stepped forward. "We would like to speak with Don ... Don whoever—"

"Cheeto Goryonli," Persil reminded her.

"We'd like to speak to Don Cheeto Goryonli and find out if anyone knows anything about the murder of my hooman aunt and the disappearance of my canine sister."

"Uh." Persil grunted and fell quiet, his whiskers withdrawing from the hole.

Pickle sank to her haunches. "My hooman aunt is dead," she told them, her voice gruff. "I'm exhausted. We've just robbed the mini-market so we could bring you guys the crap you demanded. You have to give me a break, here!" She started to pine, her keening echoing around the shop premises.

"Oh, man. Anything but that—" groaned Sal.

"Shaddappayaface!" Persil snapped. "She's grieving. Let the lady grieve. It happens, ya know? Folks lose someone, they gotta grieve." His whiskers reappeared at the hole. "Sorry for your loss."

"Thank you."

"I think, yeah, you've gotta see the Don. I tell you what I'm a gonna do. I'm a reasonable rat. Imma sort it out for you. No, really, don't mention it."

We weren't going to, thought Toby.

"Imma send Pom out. He's gonna lead you down here. Watch where you're walking, okay?"

"Okay," said Toby.

"And bring the gifts, alright? The Don will appreciate that." His voice began to fade away. "Watch your step. Watch your step."

Silence.

Toby and Pickle exchanged glances. Toby started to consider whether they'd been duped, but suddenly fresh whiskers appeared at the hole. They twitched for a moment and then, with a deep sigh, a young rat stepped out into the salon. Not all the way out, but far enough out that they could see him, his sleek brown fur and jet-black eyes.

"Are you Pom?" Toby asked.

"Pom Pagen," the rat whispered, his nose quivering like a badly set jelly. "I'm going to show you a way in." Judging by the paper-thin, whispering voice, this was the second rat from earlier.

"A way into what?" Toby asked. Were he and Pickle about to be smuggled inside the walls of the salon? What if they couldn't get out again? He wouldn't go! Not without an escape plan! It pays to be cautious.

"Don Goryonli lives down in the sewer," Pom explained, leaning away from them. "You're both too big to fit through this entrance, so I'm going to have to show you another way in."

Toby baulked at this. Clarissa would go ballistic if he returned home smelling of sewer. She'd ban him from the house for a month of Sundays. In fact, she'd probably ban him from the neighbourhood!

"There must be some other way?" he said. "Couldn't the mighty Don come out here and meet us?"

Pom jerked. "What are you saying?" he whispered. "We don't make demands of the Don. We do the Don's bidding. You must, too!"

"It's just—"

"Do shush, Toby." Pickle sighed. "Let's just get on with it, okay? This is turning into a right song and dance. It will be worth it if we get some information." She nodded at the rat. "Lead on, Pom."

Pom, seemingly reluctant, edged completely out of the hole before skedaddling to the back door. "Out," he said, and slipped through the tiny gap. Toby levitated his packages once more before nudging the door open with his nose—wide enough so his shopping could squeeze through, too—and he and Pickle followed. Toby then magicked the door closed, listening to the lock's reassuring click. With any luck, no-one would be any the wiser about the evening's events.

The rat led them down the alley in the direction of the marketplace rather than the park. At the bottom of the lane he took a left that opened onto a patch of scrubland. This waste ground had once been the site of a petrol station, but it had fallen into disrepair. Behind the tumbledown building that had once been the kiosk, there were a number of iron barrels on their sides. The rat wound his way around these to the wall that acted as a boundary for the property and stood in front of a low opening.

"It'll be a bit tight," he said.

Toby stared doubtfully at the gap, maybe eight or nine inches high and a bit more in width. He'd probably manage, but Pickle might struggle.

Pickle was beyond caring. "Let's do it," she said. Slumping onto her belly, she dug her claws into the earth and began wriggling through. When she seemed to get stuck, Toby pushed against her rump. She held fast for a moment. He pushed harder. She shot through, and he heard a squeak and a splash.

"Are you alright?" Toby barked into the gap.

"Yes, fine. Come on in! The water's lovely."

Toby doubted that, but he could hardly leave her to proceed by herself. Uttering a silent prayer for forgiveness from Clarissa, Toby gritted his teeth and went for it.

CHAPTER THIRTEEN

P*lop.*

Plop.

Plop.

Splish.

It wasn't so much that Toby had forgotten about the gifts he was holding, more that the shock of the cold water drove all rational thought and memory from his mind. For a few seconds he could only stare wide-eyed into the darkness, his entire body stiff.

But then he breathed in and began to recollect himself, his surrounds and what was going on. He quickly re-levitated the kweesh, the cheese, the biscuits and the Quavers. The Quavers were easy because the packet was floating on the surface of the water, but for the other items, he actually had to forage in the murk with his magick to bring them to the top.

Nothing seemed to have sustained too much damage, not even water damage, which was a minor miracle, but Toby put that down to the plastic packaging on everything but the kweesh. He reminded himself that whatever happened, these were gifts and *he* wouldn't be eating them. Even the Quavers.

Because ... *oooh, er* ... he found himself shoulder-deep in water unfit for canine consumption. The stink was so intense and odorous he could almost see it. Up ahead came the sploosh and rushing of water as something was emptied into the sewer.

Toby closed his eyes. There wasn't enough magick in the universe that could turn this experience into a pleasant one.

"If you can get up on this platform, it will save you wading through the water," Pom called. Toby followed the sound of the rat's voice. On both sides of the sewer was a narrow walkway. "You may still get rained on from above," Pom explained, "but it's better than swimming."

There was a splash as Pickle jumped neatly up next to Pom, but without giving the rat any advance warning, she scared him to death. He jumped out of his skin and slid sideways back into the water.

"Oops, sorry," said Pickle. "Perhaps I was a little over-eager there." She leaned over as Pom ratty-paddled around in front of her, and held out her paw. "Climb aboard."

"Huyeh! I can manage, thanks." He swam ahead a few yards and climbed by himself, keeping his distance.

"Well, *I'd* appreciate some help," called Toby. "Because I'm practically doggy-paddling already, and I have to concentrate on my packages—"

"You can't climb on my paw," Pickled pointed out. "I'll have to grab you by the collar. Come here."

Toby paddled towards her and did his best to present his neck to her. With a little huffing and puffing, grumbling and groaning, Pickle eventually managed to hoick Toby out of the water. They stood next to each other and enjoyed a good shake, the shopping shaking along with Toby. The kweesh was beginning to sound a little less pie-like and more ... mashed potato-like.

"This way," Pom called from up ahead. Pickle went first, moving into a patch of light. Toby paused and peered upwards. A streetlight shone through the grill. It offered him his first look of the sewer proper—a great oval shape with a high ceiling and numerous inlets—the colour of the water, murky brown with lots of suds that smelt oddly nice despite the other underlying malodorous pong, and Pickle. She looked like a vanilla ice lolly that has been partially dunked in melted chocolate. Where her fur was still white, it was bouffant. Where she was wet, she looked like a skinny, half-drowned ... well, brown rat, really.

What was most surprising, perhaps, was that she didn't seem to mind. She pressed on after Pom, intent on reaching their destination.

Wherever or whatever that was.

Toby, still juggling parcels in the air, hurried after them the best he could. Every now and then, one or other of the foodstuffs would careen into the wall and bounce out above the stinky miasma below, and Toby would have to rein it in. He'd never concentrated so hard in his life.

Fortunately, they weren't going far. They'd only trotted along for a couple of minutes when they came face to face with a sizable round grill above a concrete wall. The water here was directed off to the right. From here, the water must have started to flow slightly downhill because the gushing sound intensified. Beyond the grate, everything was dry.

"Who goes there?" someone squeaked.

Pom clasped the bars with his teeny little paws.

"Pom Pagen," he said. "Persil Sollozzo asked me to accompany these two down."

"A'right. Mr Sollozzo told us to expect you." A rat appeared at the grate and carefully studied both Pickle and Toby. "You're dogs, huh?"

Pickle offered the rat behind the grate a little stink-eye. "Gee! It sure looks like it, doesn't it?"

"Hey!" The rat took offence. "I don't get out much, a'right?"

He signalled to someone behind him, and a dozen rats rushed forward to grab the grate and pull it open.

Pom hurried through, with Pickle strolling after him. She bared her teeth at the grate rat and he backed away from her.

"Good morning," Toby trilled as he stepped through. "So good of you to see us."

"It's not me who's seeing you." Grate rat pointed down the tunnel. "You have an audience with the Don. He's that-a-way."

"Thanks!" Toby manoeuvred his gifts through and hustled after Pickle and Pom. Someone had lit a fire near the end of the sewer. It illuminated a big iron door, and Toby could see dozens of rats hanging around it, most of them looking anxious, wringing their paws or pacing, overgrooming or rubbing their eyes or gnawing on their tails.

Oochie.

"We need to wait here," Pom whispered.

"Will we have to wait long?" Toby asked, because quite frankly, he didn't think he had the capacity to keep levitating the packages for much longer. They trembled above his head.

"There's a queue," Pom explained, nervously gesturing at the rats gathered around.

"But ... but ... there's dozens ahead of us!" Toby said, losing the will to live. The packages plopped down beside him. If the quiche hadn't already lost all integrity, it had now.

"We don't have time for this," Pickle growled, turning on Pom in fury.

Pom held up his teeny paws and cowered away. "Please don't shoot the messenger."

"Hey, fellas! Fellas! Let's calm it all down, shall we?" An enormous rat with an eyepatch and a scar that ran the length of his face approached Pickle entirely without fear. The American accent sounded familiar. This could only be Persil Sollozzo.

"It's good to make your acquaintance!" He held up a fist to Toby first—who paw-bumped him—and then Pickle, who only curled her lip. "Persil Sollozzo.

Don Goryonli's consigliere. You're safe with me. Don't let these bums put the wind up you." He gestured at more rats, these skulking in the shadows rather than congregating by the door.

"*We're* not frightened." Pickle had decided to put him straight. "You're—"

"You're too kind." Toby stepped in. "It's good of you to make the time to see us."

"Hey! It's our pleasure. We do what we can, you know?" He beckoned to a rat loitering behind him. "Freddo. Why dontcha get some soldiers to help our guests with their gifts?"

"Right away, boss!" Freddo sprang into action. Before Toby could intervene, the packages—including his Quavers—had been spirited away. On the one hand, he wasn't sorry, but on the other, he hoped nobody else was going to claim the credit for supplying these snacks, given what he and Pickle had been through while attempting to get this far.

A boom reverberated along the sewer, there was a loud scraping, and the door opened, pushed by a dozen or so rats. A thin white rat appeared in the gap and everyone moved back respectfully. "Who's next?"

"Yoyoyoyo, Curly!" Persil yelled. "I got some

dawgs here from up top. We need to move them up the queue, you know what I'm saying?"

"Awww, come on, man!" a small black rat protested. "I've been here for hours!"

"Ey!" Persil's head jutted forward, his teeth flashing in the dim light. "Show some respect, you piece of stinking manure! You wanna see some action? I'll give you some action, you—"

The area suddenly swarmed with Persil's soldiers, separating him from the unhappy black rat and then bundling the poor creature away and out of sight.

Oh dear, thought Toby, grimacing. He hadn't meant to upset the equilibrium. He recoiled as, somewhere, the black rat's screams were abruptly cut off. "Hey—" he began to protest.

Persil's smile would have cut through an icicle. "Don Goryonli doesn't stand for nonsense," he said.

"Mr Sollozzo?" the white rat called. "Go ahead. Take your guests through."

"About time!" grumbled Pickle and made a beeline for the open door, oblivious to the multitude of rats who'd been waiting far longer than her.

Persil bowed to Toby and gestured grandly towards the door. "After you, sir."

"Sorry. Sorry. Very sorry." Apologising to the

crowd gathered around him, Toby slipped through the door, feeling the wrath of sixty or so scathing pairs of black beady eyes. *Ho hum.*

They entered what at first glance appeared to be a library of some kind, or a museum, perhaps. The light came from a flickering bulb above the door and the strategic placement of a dozen or so tea lights. Whatever this room had been used for in the past, it had been abandoned by hoomans, but the iron shelving had remained attached to the walls and become the perfect place for the rats to store their treasures. There were books—plenty of those, but most of them dog-eared and old and a little bit damp. There were all sorts of china ornaments—many missing limbs or heads—and vases with pieces broken off. There were headlights from bicycles, a bicycle pump and even a bicycle seat. There were dolls with matted hair and teddy bears with filthy fur. There were odds and ends of cutlery and a variety of canned foodstuffs, plates and bowls and mugs and beakers in every colour and pattern. A foot-high glass jar held a motley collection of beads and marbles that caught the light and sparkled. One shelf accommodated a hotpotch of odd shoes, some of which looked as though they'd been dredged up with the Mary Rose, and another had a collection of hats.

But the shelf that caught Toby's eye, and Pickle's no doubt, held an assortment of pink items. Combs, scissors, a towel, curlers, nail clippers ... and a hairdryer.

"They look familiar," Toby remarked.

"Don't they just?" Pickle agreed. "Pea thought she was going mad when she lost her hairdryer. She assumed one of our clients had nicked it."

"This way." Persil marshalled them along, a trail of soldiers following behind them. Pickle turned her head and narrowed her eyes, and a couple of them backed off, but for the most part, these little fellows were as hard as nails and weren't going to be intimidated by a filthy poodle and her scruffy schnauzer friend.

How low we've fallen, thought Toby. Could it be less than twenty-four hours since he'd won two rosettes at the dog show? *Now look at us. We wouldn't look out of place in a Dogs Trust infomercial.*

In the corner of the room, in a square space surrounded by heavily laden bookshelves on three sides, and sitting on a pink cushion on an old three-legged stool, a light brown rat sat stroking a tiny white mouse.

"Don Goryonli?" Persil said. "Your guests from the upstairs."

This, then, was Cheeto Goryonli. He looked up, his shiny black eyes appraising the newcomers. "Welcome," he said, and his voice was soft—not warm exactly, but neutral. He turned to Persil. "Sollozzo, what brings them here? Fill me in."

"Of course, my esteemed Don." Persil bowed. "They approached Pom Pagen and Salvatore Messio in the dog shop above Gate Forty-three."

"We need—" Pickle tried to butt in.

Sollozzo held up a finger. "Lady. I'm talking here, okay? You'll get your turn."

Toby gently shoulder-barged Pickle. "Ssh," he whispered. "Let them do their thing."

"But—"

"Ah-ah!" Sollozzo signalled her to be quiet by running his finger across his own throat.

Toby blinked at him. *Seriously?*

Cheeto, who hadn't acknowledged Pickle's outburst in any way, was nodding. "I know it."

I should think you do, thought Toby. That cushion had most definitely graced one of Pea's sofas not so long ago.

"They are asking for some information that they feel we might be able to provide," Persil told him.

"Mmm." Cheeto pressed his lips together and regarded the dogs with curious eyes. Toby couldn't help but shiver. There was something about this rat ... something ... dark. He oozed a kind of malevolent charisma characterised by his slow and deliberate speech and the icy way he appraised everyone.

"They brought some gifts for you," Persil added, perhaps as a sweetener.

"Did they indeed?" Cheeto's expression lifted. "Let me see."

Persil signalled to his soldiers, and half a dozen or so brought in the battered kweesh box, the slightly crushed biscuits, the packet of cheese and the family-sized bag of Quavers.

Cheeto let his mouse go. It scuttled away, diving down from the cushion and disappearing under the shelving. "You're too kind," he said, his eyes glittering. He scratched his chin with a sabre-sharp claw, and Persil nodded at his soldiers. They fell on the packets and ripped them open, but not a single one of them consumed so much as a crumb.

Toby considered this admirable. Even *his* mouth had started watering at the fragrance of the Cheddar cheese, not to mention the Quavers, even though he knew exactly where they'd been! There again, for the first time in his life, he realised that on this occasion at least, he wouldn't be jealous of anyone eating a chocolate Hobnob in front of him and not offering him one.

One of the soldiers came forward carrying what looked like the lid off a jam jar. He piled up bits of kweesh and cheese and a few shards of broken biscuit before topping the whole thing with a couple of curly Quavers. He respectfully offered the lid to Cheeto, who nodded. Another soldier stepped forward and the pair of them, with much ceremony, placed the snacks in front of their don.

Had this been Toby, and the food had been vaguely clean and hygienic, he would have fallen upon the snack with great gusto, but Cheeto was an entirely different animal. Literally. He motioned to his left. Two young rats, sleek and shiny, stepped forward. They nodded, a deep dip that was almost a bow, before each took a handful of the food from a different part of the jam-jar lid and tucked in. Toby observed this ceremony with interest, along with everyone else around him.

"What are they doing?" Pickle asked. "Why are *they* eating the food after we've been to all that trouble to get it here for someone else?"

We? thought Toby. *What does she mean by* ***we****? I've been the one practically crucifying myself to balance it in the air!* But if nothing else, he was a gentleman, so he didn't say that. Instead, he leaned into Pickle and whispered in her ear. "I think they're testing for poison."

Pickle's ears twitched. "Wow."

"Yeah."

Only when neither of the 'volunteers' had keeled over did Cheeto carefully break off a section of the goodies and nibble. He took a bite or two, then dismissed the jam-jar lid and its contents. The two volunteer rats hurriedly removed it.

Toby waited expectantly.

Cheeto's whiskers snuffled. "Very well," he said, and an audible sigh vibrated around the room as the tension decreased by a couple of notches. "What is it you would like from me?"

"We want—" Pickle started, her tone abrasive.

Toby hurriedly cut her off. "Dear Don Cheeto Goryonli." He lay down on his haunches, all the better to appear less threatening. "It's like this. My friend Pickle here is from Sweet Pea's Parlour for Pampered Pooches, which we are given to understand is part of your ..." Toby struggled for the word.

What was it? Cheeto's empire? His domain? His rat kingdom? His—

"Territory?" suggested Cheeto. He drew the word out, using all the syllables.

Toby directed a claw at him. "That's the one!"

Cheeto smiled. Rats have a devilish grin, to be sure, and for a second, Toby wasn't sure whether Cheeto was considering setting every rat in a fifty-yard vicinity on to him or was genuinely beginning to feel warm and friendly towards the dogs. Toby exercised caution and assumed the former.

"Continue," Cheeto ordered.

"Pickle's hooman auntie was murdered earlier today—" Toby hurried to correct himself. "Yesterday, now. And her sister—canine sibling—was dognapped. We fear for the safety of Candy and would love to find her." He kept his tone light, almost conversational, trying hard not to plead. "We think that there may have been witnesses from among your—" Again, Toby struggled to find the word. What? Compatriots? Fellow rats?

"Soldiers?" Cheeto asked, arching an eyebrow.

Soldiers? Glory, glory. Toby swallowed. Cheeto made it sound like he had an army of rats at his disposal. "Your soldiers! Yes!" Toby grinned around at all the rats lining the room, the ones on the bookshelves and the ones leaning nonchalantly against the door, looking for all the world like they were about to launch a full-on assault.

"Huh." Cheeto grunted, turned a paw over and studied his long claws. After a couple of beats, he nodded at Persil Sollozzo.

Persil hurried forward and ducked his head towards the Don. They conversed in low voices for a moment before Persil straightened up. "Messio?" he called.

There were murmurs and some worried squeaks before Salvatore Messio was thrust forward from his place hidden away in the corner.

"Don Cheeto Goryonli!" Sal bowed low. "Our gracious and forgiving godfather."

"Stand up, Sal!" Persil snapped. "Be a man!"

Sal hurried to do as he was asked. Toby could sense the chubby rat's anxiety from where he was standing. It pulsed out of him in waves.

"Tell our guests what you saw," Persil demanded.

"I didn't see much—"

"Tell them!"

Cheeto flicked a claw in Sollozzo's direction, and Persil quietly interjected. "You'd better have seen something, Sal. Ain't it your job to oversee the poodle parlour?"

Pickle bristled. "It's *my* job to guard the salon! You guys are—"

Toby hurried to speak over her. "The best!" he announced. "The absolute best for doubling down on the salon's security." He twerked an eyebrow at Pickle, who curled her lip in response.

Sal laughed nervously. If you've never seen a rat turn pale before, you'll just have to imagine how translucent the skin on his ears became.

Quivering, Sal turned to Pickle and Toby. "There were people," he admitted.

Persil rolled his eyes. "Ya gonna have to do better than that, Sal!"

Sal began spraying words like a machine gun. "Two people. Both men. Dressed in black. They wanted the dog!"

Pickle frowned. "Are you sure? They wanted Candy? Not the takings?"

"Why did they kill the hooman, then?" Toby asked.

"She wouldn't give the dog up." Sal shrugged. "She tried to fight them off."

Pickle sagged. "Poor Hyacinth!"

Cheeto spread his arms as though to say, and there you have it. "The lady should have given them what they wanted. They just wanted the dog. It's a tragedy. What more can we tell you?" He settled back into his seat and began inspecting his nails.

"What about a description?" Toby asked.

"Hey!" Persil swaggered towards Toby, wagging a claw up to his face. "Ya got what ya came for. Thank you for the cheese and goodbye!"

CHAPTER FOURTEEN

"Thank you for the cheese and goodbye," Toby repeated, shaking himself once more.

He and Pickle had exited the sewer near the park and had elected to bathe in the lake. Swan Lake, the locals called it, thanks to the population of ducks and geese who chose to make the park their home. It had been a long, hot summer and the water level had dropped, but recently there had been an increase in rainfall and the water was no longer as foul, as oily and thick and full of feathers as it had been in the middle of the summer.

Nonetheless, it still wasn't particularly pleasant, and the pondweed had stuck to Toby's coat. He rolled around on the grass, trying to dislodge the worst of it, Persil's final words to them lodged in his head on a loop.

Thank you for the cheese and goodbye.

Blooming rats!

Pickle, who'd been taking her time trying to wash the stink from her curly fur, clambered up the bank and plopped beside him. "I can't believe you got me into this!" she wailed. "Look at the state of me! I've changed colour!"

Toby sympathised, but he couldn't see much in the way of detail. It was still dark. He had no real idea what time it was but assumed it was around three in the morning. It had been a long night. A lonnnnnnnng night. They still had to make their way home without incident *and* avoid Clarissa's scrutiny when they arrived there.

It seemed unlikely she'd be awake though, so that was one thing on their side.

Pickle closed in on him. Toby, leaning away in case she snapped at him, slowly turned his head. The previously shining white of Pickle's coat had turned a little ... murky, maybe? Other than that, she sort of looked the same. A bit bedraggled, possibly? But if Toby knew anything about girls—and he didn't know a whole lot—he understood it wasn't the done thing to tell the truth about a poor appearance.

"You look fine to me," Toby told her. "And you certainly smell better."

Pickle sniffed at herself and blinked rapidly. "Oh, glory. I'm not sure I do."

"Trust me, you do!" Toby gave himself one last shake and, taking the beaten stone path, began trotting towards the park gate. "If you think you smell bad now, you should have caught a whiff of yourself before your dip! Come on, let's go home."

A goose waddled directly in front of Toby, turning its head to glare at him. Toby skipped over into the grass in surprise, his ears flattening, gaping in surprise at the goose.

It opened its beak and honked.

Toby took another step back. In his experience, these big park birds were wildly unpredictable.

"Beg your pardon," Toby said.

"You shouldn't be here at this time of night," the goose hissed.

"I can't disagree with you about that," Toby replied. "I don't want to be here. And in fact, I'm just leaving." He indicated Pickle, who was traipsing a long way behind, looking thoroughly downcast. "*We're* just leaving, in fact."

"Good!" the goose snarled. "Some of us are trying to get some shut-eye before they let those blasted joggers back into the park at six in the morning!"

"I appreciate that," Toby grovelled. "It won't happen again. Sorry! Very sorry!"

The goose's head jutted out at him.

Toby skipped sideways again. "Sorry!" he repeated, and called back to Pickle, who was taking her time. "Pickle?"

"I'm coming," she grumbled. "I've got half a bramble bush snagged on my undercarriage!"

"Ah." Toby grimaced. "I'd love to help you with that, but this fine gentleman wants us out of his park."

Pickle glared at the goose. "Someone needs to learn their place!"

"Hahaha!" Toby forced a laugh. "She's kidding," he assured the goose.

"No, I'm really not," she said, finally coming level with them. "And if you don't get out of my way, Goosy Goosy Gander, you'll be first choice for my Christmas dinner!"

"Pickle—" Toby interrupted her.

The goose hissed again, louder this time. Out of the darkness, half a dozen voices honked in response.

Meep. Toby swallowed. Pale faces with yellow

beaks began to emerge out of the gloom behind the original goose. Shining black eyes studied the dogs without blinking.

"Oh dear," said Pickle.

Toby wagged his tail. Just a little. A pathetic attempt to placate a flock of homicidally furious geese. "We're leaving!" he promised the first goose.

"Darn right, you are," the goose told him. "And take your friends with you."

Toby nodded and slowly sidled towards the geese. They parted the way to allow him through. Pickle stuck close by but bumped into him when he suddenly stopped and turned about. "Friends?" he queried, emphasising the *s*.

The first goose strutted away from him, perhaps six yards or so, pecked at the grass verge and sharply turned to face Toby. A fat rat dangled by the tail from his beak.

Toby squinted. Was that ...? Could that be ...? "Sal?" he queried.

"Help!" Sal squeaked, wriggling around. "Haaaaaalp!"

The goose swung his head around and whipped Sal by the tail. The rat flew through the air, looping high. It seemed almost certain he would be killed or seriously injured on impact with the ground, but out of nowhere, Pickle leapt up and snatched the rat, clamping her jaws tight.

Toby yelped in shock. "Puh-puh-puh—" he tried to say, but Pickle took off, racing for the gate.

"Oh my dog! Oh my dog!" Beside himself, Toby chased after her, leaving behind a gaggle of giggling geese.

He finally caught up with her at the gate itself. The council locked the park overnight, although there were a few gaps in the wall where it was possible to get in and out. Pickle seemingly didn't know about these. She sniffed around the gate, searching for an exit.

"Pickle!" Toby cried. "That poor rat! Why did you do that?"

Pickle turned to him, a rat tail dangling out of the side of her mouth. "Nnggh nhh hi nngh hngh?"

She gagged and spat Sal out onto the path. "Sorry. Shouldn't speak with my mouth full. Why did I do what?"

Toby stared down at Sal. The rat lay still, his tongue poking out, his little claws curled. "Why did you kill the rat?"

Pickle snorted. "I didn't kill the rotten thing. If I had, he wouldn't have a head, would he?"

Toby glanced from Pickle to Sal. As he watched, the rat opened one eye and stared up at the dogs. "Am I dead?"

"It doesn't look like it," said Toby, the relief making his knees feel weak.

"That's good," said Sal. "Cos I was kinda hoping that when I go to rat Valhalla, there'd be lots of cheese and lots of sardines and lots of cosy sheds with bench cushions and blankets to make a nest in and absolutely no cats or dogs!"

"Sorry to disappoint," said Toby. "Are you following us?"

"Did that horrible chief rat put you up to it?" Pickle asked.

"No, no." Sal sat up and began smoothing down his fur. "Ugh. Dog spit." Pickle must have had a soft jaw because from what Toby could see, the rat wasn't injured at all.

"You live in a sewer," Pickle reminded him. "Your opinion about my saliva is invalid."

"I don't generally live in the sewer," Sal told her. "I hang out below the floorboards in the salon. I have a couple of old pink towels down there. It's not bad. Bit chilly in the winter ..."

Toby closed his eyes. Would this night never end? He breathed heavily and opened them again.

"If you weren't following us, what were you doing?"

"Would you believe me if I told you I was going home?" Sal asked, waving generally in the direction of Mayflower Lane.

"No," said Pickle and Toby together.

"Oh."

"You'd most certainly travel through the sewers," Pickle said. "It's faster and safer."

"Fewer geese," said Toby. He could still hear them, squawking and honking somewhere behind them. He hoped they weren't rallying numbers so they could come after him. "We ought to get out of the park."

"There is that," Sal agreed, and tagged on behind Pickle as she followed Toby, ducking underneath some bushes and squeezing over a length of collapsed brick wall and under the hedge on the other side until they found themselves on the pavement that ran beside the main road into town.

"Well, goodbye." Toby nodded at Sal and turned away. All he could think about now was his soft, warm basket. It would probably be better for him to sleep there for the rest of the night. Clarissa wouldn't thank him for snuggling up to her in his slightly damp and smelly state. Nor would she appreciate him taking Old Joe's bed.

But that meant Pickle would have to take the sofa. He hoped she wouldn't mind.

Pickle broke into Toby's thoughts. "He's still following us."

"Huh?" They'd reached the traffic lights and needed to cross the road. There was no traffic around, but from force of habit, Toby had stopped to check and then used a little magick to press the button that controlled the lights.

Sal stood and watched them from a couple of yards away, his whiskers twitching overtime.

Toby cocked his head. "I thought you said you weren't following us?"

"Rats are liars," Pickle told him, scowling at Sal. "If he comes any further, I vote we hand him over to your friend."

"Moriarty?" Toby asked. *Ouch.* "Pickle, you're one mean girl!"

"Who's Moriarty?" Sal asked. Without any of his rat mates, he seemed smaller. Much less fierce.

"She's a cat," Pickle told him. "So why don't you just push off?"

A sudden beeping made them all jump, but it was

only that the lights had changed and the green man had appeared. *Why a man? It would be much more fun if it was a dog*, thought Toby, hurrying over to the other side, vaguely aware of Pickle's claws tapping away on the road as she followed him. *Not far now and I can have some cool, fresh water and snuggle down*, he thought. *Maybe there are some biscuits left in my bowl. A little post-midnight snack would be a wonderful thing.*

He turned into Chamberlain Drive. *Nearly home! Nearly—*

"I swear I'm going to wake up your cat friend," Pickle said.

Toby halted, afraid to turn his head. He could see Mrs Crouch's buddleia bush up ahead. It needed trimming back. Just beyond that was his front gate. So near and yet so far ...

"I told you he was following us," Pickle grumbled.

Sighing, Toby looked behind him, then pivoted.

Sal grimaced and tapped his left paw against his right paw, the long nails making a strangely crisp tsky-tappy sound. "I'm not really following you," the rat told them. "Please don't feed me to your friend."

Toby glanced around but Moriarty wasn't anywhere obvious—not that he could see too far in the dark. Nevertheless, he wouldn't put it past her to be well aware of all that was unfolding here in the street.

So much drama for one night! Toby's exasperation began to spill over. "What do you want?"

"I just wanted to know where you live," said Sal.

"So, you *are* following us," Pickle growled. "Because that's the only way you could find that out."

"Why do you need to know where I live?" Toby asked. Never mind Moriarty, he was beginning to think he'd simply dispose of Sal himself. The rat was irritating the stuffing out of him.

"I can help you," said Sal.

"Help us?" Toby asked.

"Find the people who stole your friend."

Now it was Pickle's turn to show her exasperation. "The way you helped us before?" she snapped.

"Yeah," Toby huffed. "Thank you for the cheese and goodbye."

Sal took a wary step away. "I told you what I knew," he reassured them. "But ... I wasn't actually there at the time." He sighed, avoiding their eyes. "I was er ... attending to business elsewhere, if you see what I mean. A rat has to do what a rat has to do. Ammiright?" The tip of his nose turned a darker pink.

"Ewww," said Pickle. "Gross."

"But I left Pom there."

"Pom?" Toby asked. The name rang a bell.

"Pom Pagen?" Sal reminded him. "My partner."

Toby nodded. The younger rat who had been roped in to lead them through the sewer.

"He's a young guy, sure. But I think he'll go places. Ambitious. Y'know?"

"Why do you think Pom will help us?" Toby asked.

"Because ..." Sal lowered his voice and crept towards them. "He saw what happened in the parlour. When I came back, we followed the fellas outside and up the alley. We saw the van they drove away in. Pom's pretty certain he could identify the men again. Maybe the van too. He's good with stuff like that."

"Why didn't you tell us this before?" Toby wanted to know.

"Too dangerous." Sal glanced over his shoulder, his eyes darting left and right. "You never know who's out there trying to get at us." He beckoned to Toby with his sharp, pointy foreclaw.

Toby leaned in, but warily.

Sal put his mouth next to Toby's ear. Toby winced, imagining the little teeth, sharp as needles, biting down on his lobe, but Sal only whispered, "It's gonna cost you."

Toby reared back. "Let me guess. A pound of cheese and some chocolate Hobnobs."

"No, no, no." Sal wrung his hands. "Protection. For Pom and me. We want protection."

CHAPTER FIFTEEN

Toby hadn't slept particularly well.

Now, with the sun climbing high in the sky, he lay on his back in his bed on the floor of his wizard shack, staring at the ceiling. A few weeks previously, Clarissa had bought a child's hanging mobile and dangled it from the centre strut of the roof. All the planets—including a tiddly Pluto—wobbled around the sun whenever there was the slightest breeze. Toby loved to watch them, loved the colours and the way the globes all circled at different speeds. Sometimes he magicked up a little wind—if you'll pardon the expression—so he could watch everything spinning.

But this morning he hardly saw them.

Maybe it was the lack of sleep, but his brain was whirling.

Salvatore Messio claimed to have more information than he'd first let on. Initially, Toby had found this somewhat dubious. Why hadn't he shared what he'd known when he'd had every opportunity afforded him? In fact, he'd said little even in front of his big boss, Cheeto. Given Cheeto's reputation for rough justice and reparation by homicide, Toby had found this inexplicable.

But now, according to Sal at least, he would encourage his young friend Pom to spill *all* of the beans, every single last pulse, in return for protection. It had transpired that Pom Pagen had actually been ratnapped by the Mayflower Lane Mafia when he'd been little more than a pup—who'd known that baby rats were called pups? Not Toby, that was for sure—and he wanted to go home. Back to his own ratty people.

If Toby and Pickle promised him safe passage, Pom would tell all.

Can you ever trust a rat? Toby wondered. *They're not known for playing by the rules. Not even their own rules, by the sound of it. But if Sal* ***is*** *lying and Pom doesn't know anything ... what would they get out of it?*

Toby collapsed onto his side. *And does it even matter? In the grand scheme of things, helping one rat to get where he needs to go won't hurt, will it?*

Will it?

When Pickle had questioned why Sal hadn't brought Pom along, Sal had appeared horrified. If both rats had deserted their post so soon after the dogs had visited the sewer, he'd explained, it would have been noticed. Sal had insisted that if Toby wanted Pom's help, he would have to go back to the salon under cover of darkness tonight. It would be too risky for both Pom and Sal to try to make it to Chamberlain Drive.

Toby sighed.

What was the worst that could happen? He could turn up with Pickle and the rats would demand more cheese. There might be several dozen of them, and they could, potentially, set on the dogs. However, Toby couldn't see that this would be much of an issue in reality. He had enough magick that he could see off a battalion of Cheeto's henchrats if need be.

"Tobes?" Toby heard Clarissa call from the garden. He hurriedly righted himself and attempted to appear perky.

The shed door had been left slightly ajar, and

Clarissa wrenched it open to peer inside. "There you are!" She smiled down at him and showed him a small side plate. "I thought you might like a snack."

Might like? Of course I'd like a snack! His tail thumped against the rug.

Clarissa's nose crinkled. "Phew. It's a bit whiffy in here, Toby. Have you been rolling again?" She pulled the door even wider, glaring at him.

"As if I'd do such a thing." Toby eagerly eyed the plate hovering somewhere above his head.

"Do I need to barf you?" Clarissa asked, her tone turning decidedly icy.

"No point," said Toby.

Clarissa scrutinised him through narrowed eyes. "What do you mean 'no point'?"

Oops. How much should he tell Clarissa? He hadn't considered sharing what he and Pickle had been up to the previous night. He'd endeavoured to stay out of Clarissa's way so far this morning, and Pickle was catching up on her sleep, curled up in *his* basket in front of the television, so perhaps Clarissa hadn't had to engage much with her either.

If he'd been on to something solid, perhaps he would have told his beloved hooman, but ... how could he explain their encounter with the rats? It had all been totally surreal. And then there was the small matter of the shoplifting ... There was no way that Clarissa would approve of that.

"I just mean that we'll be going out for a run in a bit," Toby explained. "I'll get all hot and dusty again."

"Sorry, mate." Clarissa placed the plate on the floor beside him. Half a slice of cheese on toast. Not just the corners, the whole half slice!

Wowsers!

"I'm not going to have time," Clarissa continued. "Rowena has been in touch with me, and she wants me to interview a wizard who lives out in the sticks." Rowena was Clarissa's boss at *The Celestine Times*. "I'm due over there in thirty minutes but it's a forty-minute drive—"

Oh dear. Probably closer to an hour, given the speed at which Clarissa tended to drive through the narrow Devon lanes.

"—and then I'm meeting Ed for dinner in Durscombe, so I might be a bit late this evening—"

Toby's ears pricked up. *Pawesome!*

"I'll leave you some biscuits in your bowl and make you some supper when I get in, okay?"

Toby whined, laying it on a little thick. Perhaps too thick, because a look of alarm crossed Clarissa's face. "I'll try not to be too late, I promise!"

"No, it's okay," replied Toby, ever gallant. "You go and have an amazing time. Don't worry about me and Pickle."

The alarm changed to suspicion. Evidently Toby was struggling to get the balance right. He stared up into Clarissa's eyes with his own full of love and —*cough*—innocence and didn't look away until at last she relaxed.

"Promise me you'll stay out of trouble," she said.

"I promise!" That was easy enough. He never ever intended to get into trouble in the first place. He surely couldn't be responsible for the sort of trouble that found him?

Clarissa reconsidered. "Or don't do anything I wouldn't do."

Toby poked his tongue out. "I don't want to do the things you do," he said, "let alone the things you don't do."

"Pardon?" Clarissa looked befuddled at this.

"Well, I wouldn't kiss DC Ed, for starters," explained Toby. "You don't know where he's been."

Clarissa smirked. "I never know where you've been and I still kiss you."

Toby couldn't deny this. "True."

"Besides, he smells a damn sight better than you do, trust me."

"Oh, I do. Implicitly," Toby told her.

She bent down and kissed his head before strolling away.

"Definitely stinky," she called over her shoulder. "Barf tomorrow."

Toby watched her go, relieved he'd distracted her from what he should and should not do while she was out.

With the coast clear, all he had to do now was wait until it grew dark.

CHAPTER SIXTEEN

Under cover of darkness, Pickle and Toby crept into the salon and quietly closed the door. Waiting for his eyes to adjust, Toby noticed that the salon had taken on a different scent. He could still smell the flowery fragrance of shampoos and conditioning treatments, but now there was a new mustiness from where it had been closed up all day. The scent of wet dog had grown stronger, emanating from the pile of damp towels that lay abandoned next to the stainless-steel bath.

There was something forlorn about the once vibrant salon, and the pair stood respectfully for a moment, until Pickle sighed and broke the spell. "Do you think they're here?"

Toby edged over to the gap in the skirting board

and sniffed it. It smelt ratty, for sure. "Sal?" he whispered. When there was no response, he tried again, a little louder. "Sal?"

"Ssssssssssh!" A hiss from somewhere close by. Toby glanced to his side. A pair of black eyes glinted at him, a little head peeking out from behind a mop and bucket combo.

"We're here," Toby told him, unnecessarily.

Sal stepped out from behind the bucket, head swivelling. "You came by yourselves, didn't ya?"

"We did," Toby confirmed, straining to see whether Sal was alone. "Is P—"

"Ssssss!" Sal placed a finger on his lips and hurried over to catch Toby by the collar. He used the collar to give himself a little leverage in order to whisper in the dog's ear. "We need to do this quietly without anyone noticing."

"Then why, in the name of dog biscuits everywhere, are we doing this where we're likely to be seen?" Toby couldn't quite get his head around this.

"Because if we desert our posts we'll be dead!" Sal explained, both front paws digging into Toby's ear. Toby stretched his neck, trying to shake the rat off. It didn't work. Sal only clung on to him more tightly. Toby had a feeling he'd be able to wear earrings after this encounter, whether he wanted to or not.

"I've been thinking about this, and we need to make it look as though you came back and attacked us."

"But we wouldn't do that," said Toby.

"I would," Pickle contradicted him. "In a flash!"

Sal shuddered.

Toby sighed. "Okay. What's the plan?"

Sal nodded and clapped his paws together. Pom edged out from behind the mop carrying what looked like a glue bottle, except the contents were red. "We're going to have a tussle," Sal said. "Make a bit of noise, drop a bit of fur—"

"Whose fur?" Pickle asked suspiciously.

Sal wobbled his head. "A bit of ours, a bit of yours—"

Pickle curled her lip. "Over my rotting corpse."

Toby intervened. "It'll be fine. Let's just do what needs do—*OUCH*!" He spun around to confront Sal, who had a sizable pawful of Toby's fur in his grasp. "What are you doing?"

"Ay!" Sal lifted his shoulders and waved his hands like an Italian cheerleader waving her pompoms. "You said you didn't mind."

Toby licked at a new bald patch just above his elbow. "You might have given me some notice!"

"It hurts less if you don't know it's coming," Sal told him.

"Is that a fact?" Toby asked crossly.

"It is." Sal threw the wads of fur into the air and allowed them to sprinkle on the floor, then looked hopefully at Pickle.

She stared at him, unblinking.

"Maybe not," said Sal. "Okeydokey. Now, next—"

Pickle growled. "What about your fur?"

"Oh, that's right." Sal laughed. "Pom, do the honours."

Pom edged towards Sal and the dogs and carefully deposited his bottle of red stuff on the floor by his feet. Reaching out, he grabbed a handful of Sal's fur.

"Wait!" Sal held up a paw and turned his head away. "Let me brace myself!" He clenched his teeth together. "Uh, right," he grunted.

Pom pulled. Hard. So hard that when Sal's fur came away, Pom careered backwards and collided with the bucket. The water inside sloshed but did not spill.

"Argh!" Sal cried out before falling to the floor in a dead faint.

Pickle exhaled in disgust.

"Amateur," Toby agreed.

"Do you genuinely think these guys have anything to tell us?" she asked. "Because this is all beginning to seem like a complete waste of time."

Sal opened one eye. "It's not. I promise."

"Get up and let's get on with it!" Pickle ordered.

Sal jumped to his feet. "Don't worry about me," he said. "Low sugar levels."

Toby ignored that. "What happens now? Is this the part where we bark and you shout and stuff?"

"Now we sprinkle a little blood," said Sal.

Toby backed out of arm's reach. "Whose blood?"

"I vote for rat blood," Pickle snarled.

Sal laughed, sounding nervous. "Don't you worry. No need for alarm. We already got this covered." He reached for Pom's glue bottle. Pom helped him prise the lid off. They had to start by peeling away some glue that had jammed the seal.

"What sort of blood is that?" Toby asked. "Because, if it's cow or sheep or something, won't your friends know—"

Sal winked. "Of course! They ain't daft. That's why this is rat's blood."

"Where did you get that from?" Toby asked, curious as to the machinations behind Sal's plan.

"Probably best if I … whooooop!" As he spoke, Sal squeezed the bottle a little too hard. A stream of liquid squirted out like a red geyser, coating him, Pom and the floor around them.

"Ewww!" Pickle backed off. "It's like a scene from a horror film!"

"*Carrie*!" said Toby, who loved his late-night horrors.

"Yeurgh," said Sal. "This wasn't quite the plan—"

"But it looks good!" Toby exclaimed. "Roll around!"

"What?"

"Roll around," Toby repeated. "Both of you! Make sure you get pawprints everywhere."

After a moment's hesitation, Sal reluctantly lay back on the floor and started squirming. Pom watched for a moment and then joined in. Toby took the bottle in his mouth and sprayed more of the blood around until the area around the skirting board—now a squirting board—resembled a rat abattoir.

"Good job!" said Toby. "Let's make some noise and get out of here!"

"Make yourself at home," said Toby, watching a damp Sal nest on one of the precious cushions in his wizard shack.

"Thanks, buddy! This is five-star luxury, ain't it, Pom?" Sal enthused. "You got any delectables to eat?"

Toby glanced regretfully up at his treat tin. "Dog biscuits," he said, and nodded at it. It floated off the shelf and settled gently down between his front paws.

He, Pickle and the rats had hot-footed it out of the salon as soon as they heard scampering behind the squirting board. "They're coming," Sal had squealed, and they'd chased out of the back door, Toby slamming it behind them, and pelted along the alley at full speed. Only then had it occurred to Toby that he had no idea what was going to happen next or what Sal had planned.

It had turned out that Sal had absolutely nothing planned, so they'd all piled back to a reluctant Toby's for a late supper.

And here they all were.

Toby shared out a few of his precious cheese-and-tuna treats before firmly replacing the lid. If the rats were still hungry after these, they could have a few of the dog biscuits left in his bowl.

Pom crouched by the door, shivering a little. Toby, unwilling to have rat blood staining his precious soft furnishings in his newly refurbished shed, and even more unwilling to confront the geese at Swan Lake again, had insisted both rats dunk themselves in his birdbath. When they'd been a little reticent to do so, he'd helped them along. By the look of it, Pom was holding that against him.

Well, it couldn't be helped.

He reached up and grabbed a towel from one of his shelves and plonked it in front of Pom. It was a threadbare one that Old Joe had probably used after his own baths in the 1970s. The pattern had long since faded to a vague shadow. "You can use that to dry off," he suggested. Pom nodded and began rolling around until his fur started to turn fluffy. It wasn't a cold night, but even after this, Pom still shivered.

Toby decided he'd have to ask Clarissa to make some hot chocolate ... *if* she ever returned home.

"Given there isn't a plan, shouldn't we come up with one?" Pickle asked, watching Sal munch his way through his cheese-and-tuna dog biscuit with the relish of a rat that hasn't eaten for at least a week.

"Of course!" Sal wiped his whiskers clean.

"These are delish. Totally delish. I don't suppose I can have another one?"

"No," said Pickle before Toby could respond. "We're getting nowhere, so you need to share some information with us and help us devise a strategy to find Candy, or we'll be turfing you out onto the road."

"Crikey! There's no need to be like that!" Sal pouted.

Toby opened his mouth to attempt to cool the rising tension, but again, Pickle beat him to it. "Spill the beans or I'll spill your guts."

This seemed a fair and uncompromising message. Sal beckoned Pom. "Come here, lad."

Pom mooched forward. Until now he hadn't said anything, but once he'd reached Sal and the older rat had a paw on his shoulder, he gave a deep shudder and began to speak in his soft, whispery voice. "I'm sorry," he said, "for not telling you everything sooner. The Mayflower Lane Mafia prefer to keep everything close to their chests, and"—he lowered his voice—"Cheeto runs the gang with a paw of steel. Plus, there are spies everywhere. You can't be too careful. Rats have been skinned alive for transgressing against the gang."

Toby and Pickle exchanged glances. "I'm sorry to hear that," Toby replied.

"I've wanted to get away from them since the first day I was forced to join. My parents, my siblings —they all belong to the West Hill mob, and I've yearned to be reunited with them." Pom swallowed. "Sal suggested that if I shared everything I knew with you, you would offer me safe passage back to West Hill and my home sewer."

Toby and Pickle communicated silently again. Pickle nodded. Toby turned to Pom. "We can do that. We said we would. But ... will you genuinely be safe from Cheeto and his crew there?"

Pom lifted his chin and straightened his spine. "I'm happy to fight and die, as long as my family is by my side!"

"So noble." Pickle, for once, approved of what a rat said.

Toby indicated Pickle should take his basket. She did so, and he settled down beside her. Addressing Pom, he said, "Tell us what you know."

Pom's ears twitched and his eyes momentarily lost focus as he thought back to the events from a couple of days ago.

"Sal had left me there, at my post, so I was on my own," he recalled. "We're always supposed to be double crewed, but it had been such a quiet day. The pretty lady with the pink hair had been there in the morning. With you." He nodded at Pickle. "But apart from that, there hadn't been anyone in. Then she left. With you." He nodded at Pickle again.

"We went to the dog show," Pickle filled him in. "At the park. We were there a good few hours."

"That's right. So, then this other lady comes in. Now we had seen her before—"

"Hyacinth," Pickle noted.

"With a dog that looks a bit like you, but chubbier."

"That's my sister, Candy," Pickle told him. "And yeah, she's into her comfort food."

"They used the big bath and lots of bubbles." Pom smiled. "I like the smell of the bubbles. Sometimes I climb up there at night and sniff around."

"Ugh," said Pickle.

Toby nudged her. "Go on. What happened?"

"Sal went off to the little rat's room. I was scooched up by the hole, sniffing the air and watching the lady comb the dog and this ... man ... barges through the front door."

"It was open?" Toby checked.

"Yes. It was a warm afternoon."

"What did the man look like?" Pickle asked.

"Did Hyacinth recognise him?" Toby wanted to know, talking over Pickle.

Pom raised his teeny pink paws. "I didn't get a good look at his face because it's hard to see that high up from my vantage point. He was wearing a dark suit though, which is a little strange given that, as I've said, it was a warm day."

Toby nodded. *Good point.*

"I don't think the lady knew him, because at first she smiled and told him that the salon was closed, but he kept moving towards her and she definitely became alarmed because she held her hands up and told him he would need to leave. He didn't leave though. He came through the little door in the counter."

"He opened it?" Toby asked, remembering how Clarissa had leaned over to do so.

Pom screwed up his face, trying to recall. "No," he said. "I remember now. It was open. The gate thing was up."

The hatch. Hyacinth hadn't secured it because she wasn't expecting clients.

"But he closed it after himself," Pom said, nodding. "Put the bolt across."

Secured it to prevent escape, Toby surmised. "Did Hyacinth have the scissors?" he asked.

Pom thought for a moment, frowning, but then his eyes lit up. "No," he said. "She had a comb in her right hand, and the left hand was empty."

"Okay," said Pickle. "Then?"

"He reached for the dog. It had been secured to the table with its leash, I think, so it needed unclipping. The man tried to do that, and the lady began tugging at his arm and shouting at him. Then another man came in. But he came in through the back! He wanted to know what was taking so long—"

"Two men?" Toby asked. "What was the second one wearing?"

This time Pom was quicker. "A suit."

"They were both wearing suits?" Pickle asked.

"The same suit?" Toby asked. "Like a uniform?"

"Not a uniform like the Parcelforce or UPS people wear. I see them coming and going all the time. No. Not like that. But, if I recall correctly, the suits were similar," Pom told them. "Same design, same colour."

"Interesting," said Toby. This sounded more and more like a professional job. But who and why?

"What happened next?" Pickle pressed.

"The second man picked something up off the bench," Pom said. "Come to think of it, that must have been the scissors, because he reached out and he cut straight through the tether on the table. The thing holding the dog in place. The first man picked up the dog—and it was whining and wriggling—and he carried her out of the back door, and the second man, the one with the scissors—" Pom swallowed.

The four creatures stared at each other, expressions bleak.

"Go on," whispered Pickle.

"The lady was clawing at him, trying to get past him to reach her dog, and he ... it looked like he hit her on the side of her head, but when he pulled his hand away, the scissors were stuck in her neck. She collapsed ... and ... I'm so sorry."

The silence that followed seemed to stretch on and on, but eventually Sal cleared his throat.

"I came back at that stage. I cut short my ... ah ... well ... I'd heard the kerfuffle and I wanted to know what was going on. Pom had ventured out of the hole. I joined him and we followed the men outside. They ran along the alley to a vehicle parked up the top on the road."

"Near the shops?" Toby asked. "Or down the market end?"

"The shops," Sal said.

"What was the vehicle? A car?"

"Not a car," said Pom. "Maybe a van thing."

"A van *thing*?" Toby asked. "What does that mean?"

"It was like a van," Sal explained. "With windows at the back."

"Did it have windows on the sides? Like a campervan?" Pickle asked. "Me and Pea went out in one of those last summer."

"It might have been a campervan," Pom said.

"If we knew what one of those was," ventured Sal.

Pickle tried to explain what a campervan looked like. "Ours was banana yellow with a big VW on the front—"

"This was black," said Sal, and Pom nodded.

"Even the windows were black," he added. "And there was lettering on the side."

Toby perked up at this. Undoubtedly, this meant that the van thing was trade, right? "What did it say?" he asked.

Pom shrugged. "I can't read."

Sal pulled a face. "Nor me."

"I remember the shapes though," said Pom. "Not the letters, but the shape of the word or image or whatever it was ... It had the same lettering as a building near the market."

"Could you draw that?" Toby asked, glancing up

to the shelf where he kept his sketchpad and crayons. The sketchpad flew through the air like a magic carpet and, after a moment, the crayons, jiggling in a mug with a broken handle, floated gently down and positioned themselves in front of Pom. Pom's eyes grew wide, and even Sal nervily licked his lips.

"How do you do that?" Sal whispered.

Toby smiled, trying to be modest. "Because I'm a wizard," he said.

Pom picked up a crayon and chewed absently on the end. Toby, afraid that the rat would eat the whole of his favourite blue crayon, cleared his throat. Recollecting where he was and what he was supposed to be doing, Pom, using both paws, made a couple of sweeping lines on the paper. The first, from left to right, curved gently upwards. The second, also from left to right, started just below the first and then curved down, equally softly. Pom lay his head to one side and studied his work of art critically before adding some downward slashes between the curved lines.

Once he'd finished, the four of them scrutinised the drawing.

Toby sighed. "Without any words, it's meaningless to me."

Pom deflated visibly.

"Aw, Pom. You did your best." Sal threw his arm around the young rat's shoulders.

But Pickle was shaking her head. "No. No. I think I know what this is!" She took the crayon in her mouth and tried to make some marks at the end of the curved lines. Giving up, she spat the crayon out. "There's a flower there. Isn't there? A lily or something?"

"That's right!" Pom brightened.

"It's the funeral directors!" Pickle announced. "The one behind the market!"

CHAPTER SEVENTEEN

"We need to go to the funeral home," Toby announced.

Clarissa, nibbling on a piece of toast while reading her emails, glanced over at him. He was standing in the middle of the rug in the front room, looking for all the world like he meant business.

"Who died?" Clarissa asked, before returning her attention to her boss's demands.

Toby spluttered. "I can't believe you said that! It's a good job Pickle's not here!"

Clarissa started. "Oh my goodness." She stared around. "Where is she?"

"Outside with the ra—" Toby choked on the word. What would Clarissa think of Pom and Sal?

"Ra?"

"Ra-ra-Rasputin!" Toby began to dance.

"It's not even half past seven, Tobes!" Clarissa rubbed her temples. Perhaps she and Ed had overdone it. Certainly, she hadn't arrived home until well after midnight. Toby was surprised she hadn't turned into a pumpkin. Wasn't that what had happened to Cinderella? She'd become a pumpkin for the rest of her life? Or was he getting his fairytales mixed up with his horror films? They all merged into one after a while.

"Is that all it is?" Toby asked. "What time do funeral homes open?"

"I have no idea. Nine? Like everyone else, I would imagine."

"Why wouldn't they be open around the clock?" Toby queried. It made sense to him. People died at all hours of the day and night. A funeral home would have to be open all hours, surely?

"Toby?" Clarissa raised her eyebrows in his direction. "I have to get a transcript of the interview I did yesterday typed up. ASAP."

"I appreciate that," Toby said, as politely as he could, "but this is important."

Clarissa's head swivelled away from the screen, her eyes burning. "I'm going to pretend you didn't say that."

But I did say it, thought Toby, somewhat confused. "I'm trying to solve the murder," he blurted.

"The murder?" Clarissa frowned. "Of Peony's sister, you mean?"

"Yes!"

"Tobes, you're such a sweetheart, I swear, but you should leave these things to the proper detectives."

"Like Ed?" Toby asked, daring to stray a little closer to Clarissa.

"Yes, exactly like Ed, although this isn't his case—"

"But that's precisely my point," said Toby, standing close to Clarissa's knee now and gazing up at her. It *hadn't* been his point, but it had *become* his point because something that should have been blindingly obvious had just occurred to him. "Think about it. Murder detectives work on murder cases."

"That's right," said Clarissa, taking a bite of her increasingly cool toast. "If the case is assigned to them."

"And dognapping detectives work on dognapping cases."

Clarissa's eyes narrowed. "I'm not sure there's a team for dognapping—"

"And there you have it!" Toby exploded. "Do you see where I'm going with this?"

"Erm—"

He stamped all four paws on the rug. "Nobody is looking into The Mysterious Case of the Missing Poodle!"

"Uh-huh."

"But if you can *find out why the poodle was dognapped—*"

Clarissa caught her breath, eyes widening. "Of course," she whispered. "Why didn't I think of that? Find out why Candy was taken and you'll find the murderer! Genius."

Toby took a bow. "Thank you. Thank you."

"Except for one small detail." Clarissa wrinkled her nose up at the remains of her toast.

"What's that?"

"We don't know that Candy was dognapped. Didn't she just run away in fright?"

Toby preened. "I *absolutely* know that Candy was dognapped. I have witnesses!"

That caught Clarissa by surprise. She lay down her toast and goggled at Toby. "Have you told the police? And what witnesses? Where?"

"I can't divulge my sources," Toby said. "They're

in witness protection." *Or on my cushions in my shed, but that counts, doesn't it?*

"Mmm."

"But I need to go and have a snoop around the funeral home."

Clarissa huffed out her cheeks. "Which funeral home? There are dozens of them in Sun Valley. This is God's waiting room, after all."

"Near the market," Toby told her, coming closer so he could turn on his baby-browns and scratch her leg.

"Ow!" Clarissa shooed him off. "Tobes, you know we've talked about your impatience before. Let me finish what I'm doing, and then we'll go."

"But that could take hours!" Toby wailed.

"It'll take far longer if you keep bothering me!" Clarissa said.

Toby sighed and shuffled towards the door.

Clarissa watched him out of the corner of her eye. "Hey."

He turned back, hoping she'd changed her mind, but she only offered him her toast corner.

Huffing, tail between his legs, he refused it and walked away.

"We're on our own," Toby announced as he entered his wizard shack.

Sal and Pom were snuggled together, curled up in Toby's basket, but now they woke up, yawning and stretching.

"What do you mean?" Pickle asked.

"Clarissa won't take us so we'll have to go alone."

"In the middle of the day?" Pickle sounded horrified. "What if the dog warden sees us?"

"I think that's unlikely," Toby told her. Pippin had often intimated that, thanks to council cuts, there were far fewer dog wardens these days than there had once been. And she ought to know, after all. She lived her life on the street.

"I'm not sure ..." Pickle hid her expression by scratching her ear.

"Looks like yer on yer own," Sal said.

"How does that work?" Toby asked. "You were the one who put me on this scent. You're coming with me."

"We can't do that!" Sal cried, totally aghast. "There'll be a price on our 'eads—"

"If your plan worked, everyone will probably think you're already dead," Pickle reminded him.

"Whose side are you on?" Sal demanded.

"Not yours, that's for sure," Pickle snapped back.

"If they see us out and about, they'll know that last night was all a set-up. They'll come after us!"

Toby considered this for a second too, then nodded. "I think it's probably best if Pom stays here —he's the one most in danger, after all—but Sal, you can come with us. We need to know for sure that the van you say you saw is the same as the one the funeral home uses, okay?"

Sal huffed and puffed, but Toby's mind was made up. He refused to let Pickle off the hook either. For sure it would take a certain amount of courage for a normally docile dog to swan around in broad daylight with neither owner nor lead, but Candy was out there somewhere, probably terrified. Faint heart never won fair poodle.

He'd promised he'd find Candy, and that's what he intended to do!

CHAPTER EIGHTEEN

Funeral home. Funeral parlour. Are these things the same? Toby had no idea. But the sign above the dilapidated building read *Carnation: Funeral Directors of Distinction*, and the flower at the end of the words was, unsurprisingly, a carnation, not a lily. In the interests of global peace, Toby decided not to mention this to Pickle, who had become increasingly jumpy and tetchy the further from home they had ventured.

Although ... not as anxious as Sal.

If a rat had been able to perspire, Sal would have been drenched. He leaned against the brick wall of the building behind them and swiped at his brow. "I'm not used to all this exercise," he said.

Neither Toby nor Pickle thought for a moment

that exercise was the problem here. Sal, poor thing, was terrified.

Carnation's was hidden away down a side street, known as Prospect Place, that led off the market. In fact, if you wandered down Mayflower Lane and took a left and a quick right, that's where you'd find it, nestled among a number of Victorian or perhaps even Georgian warehouses. At first glance, the buildings appeared run-down and unloved, but closer examination revealed that all of the units on the ground floor of each building housed one or more businesses. Most of these operated behind closed doors, with the notable exception of an owner-operated MOT centre.

Carnation's was unusual among its neighbours in that it occupied the whole of one ginormous building. Its branding, now recognisable to the dogs, had been carved in the stone that ran the length of the frontage. In addition, at the top of the three-storey building, the faint outline of the logo could be seen in flaking paint. At ground level, there was an enormous glass window which held a display of fake flowers in a marble urn that was bigger than Pickle, and a door to the left. To the left of that, a pair of old double wooden gates wide enough to allow a vehicle through was secured with a padlock and chain.

A young man in navy blue overalls, rubbing a filthy cloth over something metal, ventured out of the MOT garage and glanced idly in their direction. He didn't appear to clock them, but the dogs shrank away nonetheless. Toby realised they were too exposed, loitering across the road from the entrance into Prospect Place where they could be seen by people on three sides. "We need to get closer," he said, "and hide."

Pickle tried to dissuade him. "It's too risky."

"Nonsense." Toby waited until the mechanic disappeared into his workshop and then, after swiftly looking right, left and right again, dashed across the road and scurried behind a large green bin. Turning back to Pickle, he poked his tongue out.

Pickle sighed with exasperation, but after quickly checking for traffic, hurried after him.

That left Sal. "Hey guys! Wait for me!" He panicked and threw himself off the kerb just as a delivery truck rumbled out of the market.

"Nooo!" Toby shouted.

Pickle couldn't look. "Aaagh!" She buried her face in her paws.

"Yearrrggggggh!" screamed Sal.

The truck thundered down the road, its load crashing and banging, and zoomed straight over the rat. Toby held his breath, waiting for it to pass so he could inspect the damage. Surely there wouldn't be much of Sal left. *Oh dear. I should have taken better care of him,* thought Toby. *It's not his fault he's a dirty rat, after all.*

The truck moved away, leaving a trail of dust, exhaust and grit spiralling in the air. Through the cloud Toby could just about make out the prone form of the rat. He lay on his back, his little paws in the air, his tongue hanging out of his mouth.

Pickle peeked through her claws. "Oops."

Oops, indeed. Toby swallowed.

"We can't leave him there," said Pickle, but she made no move to go and rescue him.

That left Toby. *The things I have to do,* thought Toby, carefully checking for oncoming vehicles. Of course, there were none. The area around the market was a traffic-free zone except for deliveries and, Toby supposed, the MOT garage. How Sal had managed to be hit by the only vehicle in a two-hundred-yard radius was beyond him.

Toby reached Sal and nudged him with his snout. The rat was limp but still warm. Such a shame. Nipping Sal's tail between his teeth, Toby picked him off the tarmac and strode back to Pickle before reverently placing him on the pavement.

"Ought we to bury him somewhere?" Pickle asked. "Or do we just chuck him down the drain and let the other rats deal—"

"Don't do that!" Sal opened his eyes.

Pickle gasped. "You're alive?"

Sal patted himself down. "It looks like it."

"I thought for sure you were dead!"

"Ya don't get rid of me that easily!" Sal trumpeted, but the pale pink of his ears and nose suggested he was more shaken than he cared to admit.

"You have a habit of fainting dead away," Toby observed.

Sal ducked his head and scratched an ear. "Yeah, yeah. It's a thing. When ... ah ..." He chuckled. "When faced with danger, I kind of go a bit, erm ... weak at the knees." He pulled a face. "All four of them, in fact!"

"You pass out in dangerous situations?" Pickle clarified. "Doesn't that make them even more dangerous?"

Sal shrugged. "I wouldn't know. I never remember them."

Toby laughed. "There's something to be said for that." He smiled down at Sal. "Anyway, I'm glad you didn't get squished."

"Cheers, bud!" said Sal and looked expectantly at Pickle.

After a beat, she said, "Yeah, me too."

"Awesome." Sal had cheered up. He dusted himself off. "Listen, while you're feeling all loving and giving ... I don't suppose there's any chance you could give me a lift?"

"A lift?" Toby wrinkled his snout. "Where to?"

"No, I mean, just let me ride on your back while we're ... whatever we're doing here." Sal peeked out from behind the bin and stared along Prospect Place.

"That might hinder me if I need to do some magick," Toby said. "But I'm sure Pickle will oblige."

"Oh? *You're* sure of that, are you?" Pickle asked, but nevertheless she hunkered down on her haunches and allowed Sal to climb onto her back. "Probably best if you keep hold of my collar," she suggested.

"You da best!" Sal beamed from ear to ear.

"Let's go," said Toby. "Follow me."

He led Pickle to the next green bin and paused behind it. When the coast was clear, they made their way to the next one. The following stage proved tricky. The wide-open cavern that was the MOT garage loomed large. Music drifted out, along with the sounds of clanking and banging. There was at least one person inside, but it sounded as though there might be more.

"As long as they don't come out as we're walking past, there shouldn't be a problem, should there?" Toby whispered.

"Maybe they won't even notice us?" Sal whispered back.

"Everyone notices me," said Pickle. "I'm special."

"La-dee-dah," Toby muttered.

Pickle challenged him. "Pardon?"

"I'm singing," Toby told her. "La-da-dee, la-da-da—"

"Mmm."

Humming softly to himself, Toby edged his head around the side of the bin. He couldn't see much of the interior of the garage, but if he imagined what it looked like, he knew there would be tools. Lots of tools. And tools had a habit of ... *Oopsie!*

Clang! Clang! Clink! Bang! Clang! The harmonious music of a dozen dropped spanners and a couple of wrenches.

"Simon!" an older man shouted. "What have you done now?"

"It wasn't me!" came the response.

"Well, who the blazes was it, then?"

"Come on," Toby whispered. "While they're distracted!"

Skipping out from behind the bin, he covered the pavement in front of the open garage in double-quick time, Pickle dashing after him.

"Yeeha!" sang Sal, his claws knitted around Pickle's collar. "Ride 'em, cowboy!"

"Shhh!" Toby warned him before pelting all the way down Prospect Place, past the funeral director's, and finally huddling in the corner in front of some railings so they could all regroup.

Toby squinted up at the tall building. The top two floors had the old-style sash windows, tall and forbidding. Dust caked the glass, giving them the appearance of having brown panes. The huge window on the ground floor had probably seen a window cleaner at some stage in the past one hundred years, but not recently. The woodwork around the window was shredded, and the gilt lettering that decorated it—although resembling the Carnation branding—was hardly legible.

The double gates were in a similar state, with wood shavings scattered on the dropped pavement in front of them, the footings virtually rotted through. The most noticeable thing about these gates was the fact they were secured with a bright, shiny bronze padlock. A *new* padlock.

"It doesn't look like anyone's here," Pickle said.

"Or has been here in like forever," Sal added.

"Except this padlock begs to differ," Toby pointed out. He stretched up and nudged it with his nose. A soft click emanated from the mechanism and the clasp popped open.

Pickle's gasp sounded loud despite the kerfuffle coming from the garage. "How did you do that?"

"It's pretty basic magick," Toby admitted, nudging it again. The padlock hit the ground with a tuneful clink, and the chain slithered and zithered after it, clanking softly on the pavement and coiling around itself. "Let's go in," he said, and without waiting for an acknowledgement from his comrades, nuzzled the gate open and slunk through.

Peering through the gloom, Toby took in his surroundings. They found themselves in a double garage-come-storeroom by the look of it. There were two vehicles. One, covered in a thick layer of dust, with tyres badly in need of inflating, was a hearse. The other, enclosed within a protective sheet, had decent tyres and was taller than the hearse.

Toby grabbed a corner of the sheet and tugged. The material—a micro-porous oil-based sheeting—

slipped over the roof of the vehicle towards him and began to bury him. "Ooh-er!" Attempting to jump free, he snagged his leg and fell over. From then on, it was a losing battle. Before he knew it, he was covered in yards of the smooth, heavy material. Once Pickle had stopped laughing, she helped to pull him free. "Very wizardly," she remarked as his face resurfaced.

"Haha!" said Toby and promptly sneezed. "Dust! Ugh!"

"What does it say?" Sal pointed at the writing on the side of the van.

"Same as we figured," said Toby, studying the words. "Carnation: Funeral Director of Distinction. But it also says Private Ambulance. It must be for hoomans who don't want to share."

"What does dis-stink-shun mean?" Sal asked. "Does it clear up bad smells?"

"Only in rats," said Pickle.

Toby shook his head at her. "It means funerals for people with money, I think."

"Can money bring you back to life?" Sal asked.

"Nope," said Toby.

"Then there ain't a whole lot of point in being rich when you're dead, is there?" Sal shrugged.

He had a point.

"So, we think this is the van they used when they

dognapped Candy, right?" Toby asked. "Let's see if we can take a look inside."

"They're not going to have left it unlocked," Pickle asserted, trotting after him anyway.

"I think we've established that you're not the only dog who's *special*," Toby replied, a mite smugly.

"I'm sure everyone is special to someone," said Sal. "Except for rats. There aren't many of us who are special to anyone."

"And yet here you are with us," said Toby, examining the vehicle's back doors. There were no obvious places to insert a key, so how did the door open?

"This is true." Pickle couldn't look at Sal because of where he was on her back, but she asked, "How come you decided to leave the Mayflower Lane Mafia with Pom? You could have left him to us and stayed where you were. Surely, you've put yourself in danger by leaving the colony?"

"I've practically brought that boy up," Sal declared. "He's family."

"But—"

"He's all I have," Sal continued. "Where he goes, I go."

"And what if his real family don't want you?"

Pickle asked, as Toby pressed his paws into the metal of the car doors and began mumbling to himself.

"Then I guess I'm on my own." Sal sounded both defensive and sad, but before Pickle could ask any more, a double click from inside the van.

"Fascinating," said Toby. "You undo one lock and it undoes them all!"

"It's called central locking," Pickle told him. "It's been around since the Jurassic Age."

"Uh-huh?" Toby puzzled. "I think Clarissa's car must pre-date that."

"Can you open the doors?" Pickle wanted to know.

"Of course!" Toby waved a paw and the back doors parted ways, rather like the Red Sea. However, unlike the Red Sea, as they parted, they unleashed a tsunami. Toby's eyes widened as enormous dark shapes began to topple towards him. "Watch out!" he shouted and threw himself sideways.

Pickle followed suit, moving so suddenly that poor Sal, despite his best efforts, was unseated. Catching Pickle's rump as she bounced, he flew through the air and smacked into the side of the hearse before tumbling into the crumpled cover that Toby and Pickle had abandoned there. He lay still as chaos reigned all around and, after a moment, as was habitual, stuck his tongue out.

Toby on one side of the van and Pickle on the other looked on in silent horror as what they initially mistook for furniture spilled from the rear. Polished wood? Red cushions? Not cushions ... Kind of cushions ... Cushions inside the wood. *What in the world?*

The first thing hit the concrete floor with a disturbingly loud thud and its lid slid sideways. Without pause, the second thing tumbled down on top of it. Now there was no mistaking what Toby was seeing.

Coffins!

He took another step back, recalling the time he'd been chewing on what he'd thought had been butcher's bones but may, in fact, have been zombie bones. *Eww!* He wasn't ready for more corpses.

However, as the dust settled, it became apparent that in this case, fortunately, the coffins were brand new and didn't harbour any occupants.

In total, five coffins slid out of the van, three of the lids becoming dislodged, the other two remaining in place. A sixth coffin slid halfway out and rested on top of the debris.

"Whoops," said Toby. "That was a little unfortunate."

"At least there aren't any dogs inside," said Pickle.

"I should try and levitate this lot back," said Toby. "The thing is, it might be a bit heavy for me." He glanced around. "Where's Sal?"

"Over there," said Pickle, gesturing towards the prone rat. "He's 'dead' again."

"Hmm. He—"

Toby didn't get any further. The distinct sound of a car pulling up directly outside whipped the words out of his mind. "Someone's here!" he hissed.

Pickle crouched, as though this would prevent her from being seen.

"Sal!" Toby hissed. When the rat didn't move, he called louder. "Sal!"

This time the rat must have recognised the urgency in Toby's tone because he sat up. "Wassup?"

Outside, feet crunched on loose stone chippings. "Did you forget to lock the place up again, Ryan?" A man's voice. Annoyed.

"Of course not!" Another man. Ryan, probably.

The first man cursed. "We must have had a break-in!"

"They're going to come in. We need to hide." Toby edged away from the van, catching the floating edge of one of the coffin lids, already perched precariously on top of a coffin. It swayed for a moment before sliding onto the floor with a loud clunk.

"It sounds like there's someone in there!" Ryan whispered.

The first man growled in response. "Well, get in and check it out!"

"You go in and check it out! What did your last slave die of?" Ryan complained.

"I stabbed him in the back and then slit his throat!"

Oof! Toby's eyes darted left and right. These guys didn't sound like they were messing.

Sal crept a little closer to Pickle, reaching out to grab a handful of fur. "Hide!" Toby ordered, and the three of them moved as though someone had lit a firework under their backsides.

CHAPTER NINETEEN

"Kids?" Ryan suggested.

"Could be," the second one agreed. "Doesn't look like anything's been taken."

"Messing around. Nothing else to do." Ryan was moving around. His voice came from different directions. "There's no need for it, is there? Gainful employment. That's the answer."

"Remember how Grandad always used to say they should bring back National Service. Short back and sides and a kick up the arse. That'd sort them."

"Yeah. No damage done by the look of it," Ryan said, his voice closer.

"Just vandalism. At least there's no bloody graffiti anywhere." The second man hadn't moved at all.

Not as far as Toby could tell, because, well-hidden, he couldn't see what was happening.

"Maybe they didn't have time," Ryan replied. "Maybe they're still here."

Toby held his breath. Beside him, Pickle shivered.

"Mmm." This time, the second man did make a move. "I'm going to look inside the office and upstairs. You clean up in here."

Ryan grunted. "I can't move all these coffins by myself."

"Of course you can. There's nothing in them," the first man scoffed. Keys jangled.

"I don't want to be blamed for any damage!" Ryan said.

"Relax, Ryan! They're props." A door opened. "They're not going to be used! It doesn't matter if they get a bit scratched." His voice began to recede. "She'll never notice."

Ryan grumbled inaudibly for a moment. "Alright. Come on," he muttered to himself.

The earth moved for Toby. And Pickle and Sal come to that. The three of them had hopped into the back of the van—Sal had required a helping paw—and climbed into the only remaining coffin. Toby had just had time to levitate the lid so that it had snapped neatly back into place over them before the two men walked in.

Ryan had evidently decided to start by moving their coffin securely back into place in the van. "Heck." The coffin stopped sliding. "Feels like there *is* someone in this."

Toby's heart beat hard against his chest wall, so loud he worried that Ryan would be able to hear it.

"Lionel?" Ryan called from a little further away. "Lionel?"

When no answer appeared to be forthcoming, Ryan cursed and roughly pushed the coffin all the way inside the van. "It's not my problem, is it?" he grumbled. "Let him sort it out."

More clattering. The van shook. Something solid slid in beside Toby's coffin. Another coffin, no doubt. Ryan methodically loaded each coffin, two across and three up by the sound of it.

The dogs were well and truly trapped.

"How are we going to get out?" Pickle hissed, but Toby couldn't answer her. At this stage, he didn't have the foggiest idea.

"Eurgh!" Ryan was still complaining.

"Shall I give you a hand?" Lionel had returned.

"I've done it now!" snapped Ryan.

"Easy, bro," Lionel counselled. "You'll get yourself worked up into a right tizzy, and we both know that's not good for your blood pressure." He laughed.

"Knock it off," grumbled Ryan. "Is there much damage upstairs?"

"None at all. No-one's been in there. Must've been kids like we thought." Lionel sounded satisfied. "Right. Let's go. Do you want to drive this or the Merc?"

"Drive it where?"

"She wants us to take it up to the house. I'm guessing she's got another job for us."

"She wants us to take the van out again?"

"She probably doesn't want dog hair in the back of her precious car."

"Then what was the point of me loading all those bleeding coffins into the back? I'll have to take them out again—"

"They're props, Ryan. You know that."

"But it makes more work!"

"We just do as we're told. Remember?" Lionel laughed. "Play the game and take the money. That's all there is to it. Better than working on that awful fishmonger's stall on the market, right?"

"I suppose." Ryan didn't sound convinced. "Only ... I didn't like what happened to that woman in the grooming place—"

Pickle made a small noise. Toby crushed what he thought was her front paw with his, reminding her to stay quiet.

Sal made a choking noise.

Oops. Toby moved his paw away.

"These things happen." Lionel sounded cavalier. "Merc or van?"

"I'll take the Merc," Ryan said. "Driving this van is too maudlin. It makes me think of dead people."

Keys jangled once more. "Lock up after me," Lionel ordered. "And make sure you do it properly this time! I'll see you at the house."

Toby considered their options. With another two coffins piled on top of the one the dogs and Sal were hiding in, they were going to be hard-pushed to find an easy way out. Perhaps he could summon up enough magick to blow a hole in the side—

The van vibrated and then the engine roared noisily into life.

Too late for any sort of plan. They were on the move.

CHAPTER TWENTY

"I feel sick," complained Sal for the umpteenth time.

"It'll all be over soon," Toby told him. He'd lain down and closed his eyes. There didn't seem much point in doing anything else, and closing his eyes for a rest could be as good as proper sleep sometimes.

Sal groaned. "You said that before and we've been driving for days."

"It's been about ten minutes," Pickle pointed out. Perhaps she'd been counting the seconds. "Maybe twelve." Or perhaps she hadn't.

"I think we've been heading out of town," said Toby.

"That seems blindingly obvious," Pickle sniped.

"It's a titchy town. It doesn't take long to get out of it!"

Toby decided not to argue. She was right, of course. You could easily escape from Sun Valley in a few minutes. But he'd also been tracking left turns and right turns and the uphills and downhills, and he had a feeling they were travelling east. He couldn't have sworn to it, but the steep hill followed by a long straight had persuaded him of that.

That told him they wouldn't be travelling a long way. There were only a few towns and villages accessible using the coastal road. If you wanted to go further east, you would normally travel inland and get on an A road or the motorway.

He was right. After another minute or two, the van made a hard left and the road became bumpier. It slowed but kept on making progress for another mile or so, labouring as it climbed another hill.

Eventually, all movement ceased. The engine idled for a few seconds and was then turned off. The driver's door opened and closed, and footsteps receded into the distance.

Pickle breathed a sigh of relief. "Can we get out of here now?"

"It might be wise to wait a little longer," Toby suggested.

"Surely there's no time like the present?" Sal squeaked. "I'm getting claustrophobic in here!"

"Just a few moments," Toby replied. He badly wanted to get out too, but he stood firm.

He was right to. In moments, they heard a car pull up alongside the van. The Mercedes, no doubt.

"Lionel?" Ryan called as he clambered out of the car.

The footsteps returned. "Put the van in the barn, will you?" Lionel ordered. "Keys are still in the ignition."

"Why me?" Ryan grumbled. "Why can't you do it?"

"She wants to see me. Now."

"Doesn't she want to see me as well?"

"Why would she?" Lionel asked.

Harsh, thought Toby, wondering who 'she' might be.

"Because we're partners, aren't we?" Ryan whined. "That's what you always say!"

"And it's true. It's true, baby brother of mine," Lionel soothed. "Why don't you come and find us when you've parked the van up in the barn. We don't want anyone to see it here, do we?"

"No, I suppose not."

"Grand." The footsteps started away once more.

"Oh, and while you're at it, empty it out, will you? Apparently, we're going after a golden retriever tomorrow, so we'll need the space."

Toby raised his not-insubstantial eyebrows as he listened to the stream of obscenities that followed this announcement, but despite this outburst, Ryan proceeded to the front of the van and climbed in. The engine started up once more and, after a little toing and froing, a pause where the engine idled, where Ryan jumped out and then back in, followed by a little more toing and froing, the handbrake was pulled on and the engine stopped.

Ryan made his way to the rear of the van and opened the doors. "Blasted coffins. Load them. Unload them. Load them. Unload them. Do this. Do that. What does he think I am?" he moaned. "Why are we even bothering? The wages aren't that great. I could have gone to university. I could have made something of myself. I should never have listened to him. What are we but the paid lackeys for some old dear, someone we rarely see, who's as shady as—"

On and on it went as Ryan unloaded the coffins. However, despite his evident frustration with life, the universe and everything, he was remarkably gentle with the load. Toby heard far less banging, clunking and scraping this time. The coffin lying directly above was removed, followed by the one to the side of them. Now was the moment of truth, because hadn't Ryan previously been concerned there was something in their coffin?

"Let's spread out." Toby hurried to the feet end of the coffin, leaving Pickle at the head end. "Make like a dead weight," Toby whispered to her and Sal.

"A dead weight? I weigh nothing, me!" Sal said.

"Just think heavy thoughts!" Toby urged him, deciding not to share with Sal that he was by far the fattest rat Toby had ever seen.

As Ryan began sliding the coffin out, Toby willed the man not to notice the extra weight. Perhaps it worked. Although he grunted and groaned, Ryan didn't complain this time. The coffin wobbled a little before settling, presumably on top of another one.

Job done, the rear van doors were slammed, and the van beeped as Ryan locked it remotely.

So posh, thought Toby. *Clarissa needs this magick key!*

A moment later he heard a distant clunk, and then silence fell.

Sal shifted restlessly. "Can we get out now? I think I'm seasick."

"Do *not* chuck up in here!" Pickle ordered. "Wait until we get out."

Sal moaned.

"More to the point, *how* are we going to get out?" Pickle asked.

"It's simply a case of lifting the lid," Toby told them. "I can do that with some levitation." He closed his eyes—it was pitch dark anyway, so it made no difference—and imagined the lid lifting off, somehow effortlessly, simply floating upwards calmly and quietly ...

Unfortunately, it didn't quite happen that way. The lid shifted but hardly lifted, although it did allow a slither of light in. It creaked and groaned and dropped back down with a thump.

"Try again," said Pickle.

"Hurry," said Sal. "My tummy is rolling."

"Mine too," said Toby. "I'm famished. Could really do with a sammich about now."

Sal made a strange noise. *Bwaaarrrk!*

"Hurry!" Pickle urged Toby.

"I think you'll have to help me." Toby began summoning energy from deep inside his core.

"How? I don't do magick!"

"You don't need to do magick," Toby told her. "Just push with your head."

"Oh."

"Three two one ... go!"

Toby pushed with his mind while Pickle hunched her shoulders and pushed with her back and head. "Yeeeurggh!"

At first, Toby thought he would fail again, but by straining every nerve and fibre in his being, finally the lid of the coffin slid sideways, flooding the interior with light. The three animals blinked and winced, peering around at the old stone barn they found themselves in, complete with the odd hole in the roof and gaps in the wooden shutters and doors.

"Phew." Toby stretched. As he did so, he knocked the coffin lid. It tilted on one edge.

"Do we really want that to fall—" Pickle started to say. "Oh. Too late."

The lid crashed to the ground, the noise rolling and echoing around the barn like thunder.

"Unfortunate," said Toby. "Let's hope no-one heard that."

Sal could take it no longer. He clambered up the side of the coffin and threw himself overboard. Pickle and Toby averted their eyes as the poor rat found a place to expel his breakfast.

"What now?" Pickle asked.

Toby took a deep breath. "I think we should go and explore. Don't you?"

CHAPTER TWENTY-ONE

Once Sal had recovered—"I don't ever want to climb inside a moving shed again," he'd complained—escaping from the barn posed no real challenge for the intrepid trio. The barn wasn't in the best shape to begin with; the holes in the roof let in both sunshine and rain, and the gaps between the planks of the wooden shutters and the holes in missing chunks of the crumbling exterior walls encouraged a flow of air. Antiquated farm equipment—things with enormous rusted spikes, ploughs and hoes, harnesses and yokes for horses or oxen—must have been half-buried among the rotting bales of hay for over a century.

Toby and Sal scrambled under a ramshackle door easily enough, but Pickle had a bit of squeeze. By the time she made it to the other side, she was covered in straw and a thick layer of dried dust. "Splendid," she said, shaking herself to no avail, but at least sharing her detritus with Sal and Toby.

Toby gazed around at their new surroundings. He'd been right about their direction of travel. The scent of the sea tickled his nose. They couldn't be far away. However, all he could see was a mix of farmland and forest. The lane that presumably led to the main road was off to the left, travelling down the hill, while to their right, up a stone track, stood an imposing country house.

"Is that a castle?" Sal asked, his eyes wide with wonder.

"Maybe a department store," Pickle suggested, whose knowledge of buildings pretty much started and ended with what was available in town.

"Or a palace?" Sal queried.

"I think it's just one mighty huge house," said Toby.

"Wow!" Sal breathed out in awe. "How big does a family of hoomans need to be to live in a house this size?"

"Scarily big," Toby decided. He hoped they wouldn't run into any of the residents, but the more there were, the more likely it was that they would. That was slightly worrying.

"It looks like a block of flats that's fallen on its side," Pickle said. "Our flat above the salon has three rooms. That's plenty. How many does this have?"

"Your guess is as good as mine." Toby stood beside her, the pair of them counting all the windows they could see, but there were too many and they kept coming up with different answers. The house, almost submerged in a creeper of some description but with sneak peeks of browny-gold stone beneath, had three floors, with a mock Greek entrance and a couple of enormous stone urns arranged around a wide terrace. As the three of them ventured closer, the signs of decay became more apparent. The cracked and crumbling stonework, the faded paint, the patchiness of the roof, the age of the windows and the accumulated filth; it all spoke of years of neglect.

But perhaps most unnerving of all? The complete silence. There should have been birds—sparrows twittering among the creeper, tits nesting in the rafters. At the very least there should have been seagulls circling overhead, high up on the thermal currents.

Toby, as attuned to nature as he was, noticed the

absence of the birds almost immediately, but it took a little longer for Pickle to work out what felt wrong.

She shivered. "Why so quiet?" she whispered.

"Maybe there's no-one here." Sal was huffing and puffing a little from walking up the slope. Without hesitation, Pickle hunkered down and offered him a ride.

"We know at least three people are here," Toby reminded them. "Lionel, Ryan and whoever the 'she' is they've been talking about."

"An old woman," Sal agreed. He had been listening to the brothers' conversation, then. From the safety of Pickle's back, he peered around. "Would one old woman really live here by herself?"

"I suppose her family might have all moved away," Toby said. "Perhaps her husband died ..." But he was making it up. Concocting a story to help them all feel better. To make the whole situation somehow *normal*.

They crept closer to the entrance, along the crumbling terrace. There were no lights in any of the windows, but perhaps that wasn't so unusual given that it was broad daylight. The front door may once have been framed by cultivated roses, but now these were wild, although still with their own unruly beauty.

There should have been bees ...

Toby studied the stubbornly closed front door. "I think we should look for a different way in," he whispered.

"Why are we going in at all?" Sal squeaked. "It might be dangerous!"

"You heard what they said about the golden retriever," Pickle reminded him. "We've found the right people. These are the men who murdered Hyacinth and dognapped Candy. Candy might be here. We could find her!"

"Sssh!" Toby hissed. Pickle's indignant voice carried on the otherwise silent breeze. He would prefer no-one was alerted to their arrival. "Come on. Follow me."

They gave the front door a wide berth and crept around the side of the house, passing a greenhouse that must once have been as grand as the house itself. Now, devoid of most of its glass panels, it remained an interesting structure because, inside, plants continued to grow, wild and free. Branches, stems, bushes and fronds tangled and entwined, locked together in harmonious chaos. The grass surrounding the greenhouse grew long, too, a lawn that had now returned to weed and wild grasses.

There should have been butterflies and crickets

and woodlice and worms and all manner of insects, and yet ... there weren't.

A fist clenched in Toby's stomach—a feeling of dread sitting heavier and heavier the more progress they made towards the rear of the house. Off to the left was a structure, more or less collapsed, that might once have been stables. It had been a long time since any horses had grazed or whinnied there, however.

Three-quarters of the way along the rear wall of the property stood a wooden lean-to—although it was doing more leaning than standing—surrounded by the remains of a kitchen garden. They approached this area quietly, wary of anyone who might be watching out of the numerous rear windows or about to exit through the back door.

Sal made a sudden guttural noise.

Toby turned to him. He sat stock still on Pickle's back, his spine straight, his ears pricked. He lifted a paw—a shaking paw—towards the lean-to. His mouth opened but he'd been struck temporarily mute.

Frowning, Toby squinted back at the lean-to. What were they looking for? There were pots for plants in the windows, some old curtains flapping in the breeze and some bits and bobs hanging from the window frames ...

Toby recoiled as he suddenly realised what he was seeing.

The bits and bobs hanging in the windows that he'd initially mistaken for empty macrame plant hangers—the type favoured by Mrs Crouch in her greenhouse—were nothing of the sort.

"Are they—" Pickle swallowed. "Are they what I think they are?"

"Yes," Toby whispered. Rats. Dead rats. Hanging by their tails.

"Ohhhh!" Sal wailed and fainted dead away.

"Am I alive?" Sal blinked.

"Of course you are," Toby reassured the rat as he came round. He and Pickle had carefully carried Sal over to some bushes, where the three of them could hide and watch the back door. This location had the added advantage that they could no longer see the lean-to.

Or its horrendous bunting.

Sal clasped a paw to his forehead. "I don't think I can go on. My heart beats ever fainter."

Pickle sighed. "You're so melodramatic."

"To be fair, I think I'd be a bit shaken up if I saw" —Toby mouthed the words—"dogs hanging by their tails"—and jerked his head in the direction of the lean-to—"over there."

"Mmm. Fair point." Pickle nodded.

"I don't want to die!" Sal jerked upright. "I just want an easy life. Plenty of food. Maybe a wife. A couple of dozen children. A thousand or so grand-children. It's not much to ask."

"Wow," Toby said. "When you put it like that—"

Sal threw himself in front of Toby, clawing at his chest. "Take me home. *Please*! I'm too young to die! Take me home, I beg you!"

"Relax," Toby soothed him. "We won't let anything happen to you, will we, Pickle?"

"What?" Pickle had tuned out, watching the back of the house for movement. "Oh. No. I suppose not."

"Waaaaah!" Sal sobbed loudly.

"She won't! I won't!" Toby told him, his voice firm.

"I think I've worked out how we can get in." Pickle cut through the ongoing drama. "Look. See there?" She gestured with a paw. Sal stopped sobbing as Toby leaned closer to Pickle to take a look.

"What's that?" Toby asked, studying a wooden door, not much taller than him. "Is it a dog flap?"

Pickle snorted. "After a fashion. I think they call it a coal bunker."

"Yes! That's right!" Toby wagged his tail in excitement. "I've read about those. The coal merchant would come along with his sacks and dump coal into your cellar or your outhouse."

"This must be a cellar, then." Pickle eyed the wooden covering. "I reckon you can lift that lid off with your magick ... but if you can't, then I suppose I might be able to prise it off with my teeth."

"It looks pretty battered from here," Toby agreed. "Let's go and investigate!"

"Wait!" Pickle's gaze swept the back of the house once more. Not a hint of movement. "Alright. Jump on, Sal. Avert your gaze. We're going for a ride."

Sal did as he was bid, burying his face in Pickle's dusty fur as they scurried past the lean-to, heading for the square of wood beyond. Pickle had done well to spot it, given the amount of overgrown shrubs and weeds growing up the wall of the house. Toby used his teeth to prise away the worst of the tangle and stared at the slab of wood with interest. Obviously, back in the day, the original would have been sturdier, but this was a more recent replacement forged from MDF. Rain damage had taken its toll, causing the wood chips to swell and the seams to split. Even more fortunately for Toby, the long, hot summer had dried the bunker cover into a husk, just ready to fall apart. He scratched at the surface, but this was the toughest part, so instead he placed a paw dead centre of the square. "*Fragor*!"

A small explosion. A puff of soot. The square of MDF crumbled into what looked like dry gravy granules and pooled at Toby's feet. "Pawesome!"

Sal slid from Pickle's back and peered into the resulting entrance. "Hellooooo?" he called.

"Helloooo—oooo—oooo!" echoed back at him.

"A cellar," Sal announced, crooking his head to listen more intently. "Can't hear any of my kin or cousins, though."

Pickle joined him to squint into the gloom. "How far down are we going to have to drop, I wonder?"

Toby joined them. "More than a couple of feet but not quite to the centre of the earth, I should imagine."

Pickle glanced sideways. "You're so full of it, do you know that?"

"Of course!" Toby smiled, certain she meant magick. Or wonderfulness. One of the two.

"Who's going first?" Pickle asked, and without

waiting for a response, backed away slightly and pushed Toby headfirst through the gap. "Schnauzer in the hole!" she sang.

Crump.

"Oof!" Toby landed on his side, the air exploding from his lungs. He scrambled to sit up, but the rubble beneath him made that difficult. He could only slip and slide with every move.

"How far down is it?" Pickle called.

Toby tipped his head back. He could see both Pickle and Sal silhouetted against the sky. "Excuse me! You could have killed me!"

"And yet, still you breathe," she muttered before raising her voice again. "How far?"

"Only about four feet, if that." Toby looked around. Perched on a mountain of coal, he realised that you could fall a good deal further if you came through at the wrong angle. "Erm ... as long as you land in the same place I did."

Pickle picked Sal up by his tail, leaned into the hole and dropped him. Toby hurried to catch him but angled himself incorrectly, lost his footing, rolled over and ended up with the rat landing on his belly.

"Oof!" he said again.

Sal trampolined off Toby's belly and landed gracefully on the cellar floor.

"Watch out, I'm coming in," Pickle called, and the next moment landed beside Toby with a thud, slipping and sliding on the pile of old coal, too. "Ooo-er," she said and roly-polied down the mini-coal mound.

As she clambered to her feet, Toby glided down to where she and Sal waited for him.

"Look at the state of you," Pickle said.

"Look at the state of yourself!" Toby replied.

Pickle did so and wailed. "Why am I black?"

"It's coal dust," Toby reassured her. "It'll wash off." He had no idea whether it would or it wouldn't, but it sounded like the kindest thing to say.

Sal rubbed his fur, spreading the dust around. He had the look of a rodent who'd been roasted in a fireplace, so sooty and bedraggled was he. "I'm beginning to wonder what I've let myself in for. This has been quite a day so far."

"And it isn't over yet." Pickle lifted her chin, the light of determination burning in her eyes. "If Candy is in this house, it's our duty to find her!"

"We'd best press on then," said Toby.

CHAPTER TWENTY-TWO

Everything that could creak did so.

Everything that could groan did so.

And not just the dogs' stiff muscles, but every part of this old, forgotten house.

The stairs out of the cellar creaked and groaned, whined and protested with every step the dogs took. Sal, riding on Pickle's back once more, kept a tight hold of her collar, his eyes straining to see, his ears listening out for the slightest response to the amount of noise they were making despite their best efforts to move stealthily.

They took it slow, striving to minimise their presence in this vast house. At every new obstacle they paused and took heed and, even if they felt it was safe to continue, still they listened before eventually a twist in the bowels or a speeding heartbeat spurred them forward.

The door at the top of the cellar stairs opened easily enough with just a word from Toby and a push from Pickle. They found themselves in a long corridor, worn brown linoleum beneath their feet and mustard-coloured walls that did little to dispel the air of gloom. Above their heads, naked bulbs hung from wires but cast no glow.

The thickness of the dust in the air seemed to deaden sound. The gentle tip-tap of four pairs of paws made almost no impression in this closed-up tomb of a dwelling, and perhaps that was a good thing. Toby scanned left, then right. To his left, half a dozen closed doors. To his right, more doors but the promise of something else. He could make out the balustrade of a curling staircase.

He wanted to go that way, not least because there was more light in that direction, whereas here, at the back of the house, the stuffy air stifled him, but Pickle's ears were twitching, her attention captured by something to the left.

"Let's go this way," she whispered, and Toby, committed to exploring the whole house if necessary, nodded, following after her.

They paused at each of the closed doors, dipping

their heads to the gap between floor and door and listening intently. Not a breath of sound. Not anywhere. If Candy inhabited one of these rooms, surely she could not stay so quiet?

They padded on, hardly breathing, until they came to the final door. This one wasn't locked. Pickle pushed, gently, gently. The door creaked and swept away from them, clattering against the wall behind. For a fraction of time, the room appeared bathed in light—a welcoming golden light. A man sang. A woman laughed, more of a giggle. A dog barked. Meat sizzled on a skillet. Pots clanged. As one, the three animals lifted their noses to breathe in the fragrance of thick, fatty, smoked bacon and ...

And just like that ...

All gone.

Dumbfounded, Toby paused at the threshold, his gaze sweeping the expansive room in front of them. This had been a kitchen. A range still remained at one end, a fireplace at the other. But no fire burned. No meat sizzled. No woman sang, and no man laughed.

The faintest of barks.

Pickle barged into the kitchen, upturning a pile of bowls that clattered and smashed as they scattered. Toby hurried after her.

They had time to see a dog turn to face them, something small. A Jack Russell, perhaps. It opened its snout to bark again, to see them off … and …

And faded away in front of their eyes before they could react to it.

The dogs pulled up, side by side, panting noisily. "What happened?" Pickle whispered.

Toby pivoted. A shadow by the range …

And gone.

"Ghosts," he murmured. "Nothing to worry about." And yet, the thought shook him. He couldn't see ghosts. Wasn't blessed with that ability. Not yet.

Pickle shivered and partially retraced her steps.

A creak from above.

The ceiling? Or perhaps the wooden boards of the first floor. This was the first sound they'd heard that hadn't originated from something they themselves were doing. It reminded them that despite appearances, they were not alone.

Satisfied that the kitchen would yield nothing to assist them, Toby led Pickle—Sal still on her back—past the smashed crockery and out of the kitchen door. Back in the corridor, he became aware of more shadows. Pausing, he watched as they flitted back and forth, rather like the shapes cast by a candle against a bare wall.

Nothing to worry about, he repeated under his breath. They pressed on towards the hall and the stairway, eyes like saucers, searching every nook and cranny for something that might surprise them or cause them harm, but there was only dust and dirt, tatty old spiderwebs and dead insects. They might have been inhabiting a nightmare. An endless, silent, gloomy corridor with countless numbers of identical doors ...

But then ... a gentle tinkling sound.

Followed by a harder chord.

Someone playing a piano?

The closer they drew to the entrance hall, the lighter the house became and, much to Toby's relief, the fresher the air. As they reached the end of their corridor and drew level with the entrance into the hall, Toby realised that there was an identical corridor opposite, however, the music itself was coming from close by—a room opening directly from the hall to the right of the front door.

Once, this house would have been grand, but now it was a shambles. The staircase curled up and away from the entrance, an enormous chandelier dangling down with much of its glass missing, shards collecting on the marble floor. The floor, heavily pockmarked and encrusted with dirt, would once have been a shining grey, white and black masterpiece, but it hadn't been swept or washed for far too long.

Toby turned his attention to the room with the music. The door stood slightly ajar. Light spilled from it, casting a gold shadow on the filthy marble floor.

Licking his lips, Toby nodded at Pickle, and together they stole over to peek through the open door. A burst of laughter, men and women chuckling together. A chandelier—complete and sparkling—threw its silvery illumination over a shining grand piano where a young man in immaculate tails played, his shoulders moving with the emotion of the music, his long, refined fingers brushing lightly over the keys. An enormous fire blazed and crackled in an elegant fireplace. A woman in a pale blue ballgown swept past them, blocking their view and then ...

The chandelier blinked out. The piano lid slammed closed. The fire roared once ... and died away.

Toby edged into the room. Everything he'd only now witnessed had disappeared. The fireplace had been stripped of its glory. Pigeon bones, or something of that size, roosted in the grate among dried-out nests and desiccated leaves. The piano had collapsed, sunk in the middle, its wires and keys splayed out like the ribs of a skeleton. This piano hadn't played a note for decades.

The windows were shuttered, but here as everywhere, even these had rotted and the fingers of the late afternoon sun found a way to filter through. Toby observed as Pickle sniffed along the skirting boards, Sal leaning over her head to watch. Drawing a blank, Pickle shook her head and padded back to Toby.

"Down the other corridor or upstairs?" he whispered.

Pickle lifted her eyes skywards.

Toby understood her train of thought. They knew someone was upstairs, at least. He nodded, and together they tiptoed back into the hallway ...

Where only moments before, the front door had been firmly closed.

Now, it stood ajar.

Toby gaped at it. *Did someone walk in or leave? Did they pass us? Did they* ***see*** *us?*

And where are they now?

CHAPTER TWENTY-THREE

Toby's heart fluttered. He'd been involved in a few adventures in his short life, but nothing quite as weird and unnerving as this. Why, one moment, could he see the rooms as they might have been and yet the next, the house was practically reduced to a hovel?

"I didn't hear anyone out here, did you?" Pickle whispered, eyes locked on the open door. "You'd have thought we would."

Toby agreed. The floors were marble. It was impossible to remain quiet unless you were barefoot perhaps, or wearing big fluffy socks and you were using the hallway as a skating rink, but even then you'd disturb the debris. After hurriedly checking the corridors, he edged towards the open door and gazed out. From here, the land fell gently away. The Mercedes remained where Ryan had parked it. There was no other vehicle in sight.

She knows we're here.

The thought lit up like a neon sign in Toby's head. He didn't quite understand what it meant. Who knew he was here? The mysterious old woman? And how did she know?

Pickle cleared her throat.

Toby stepped away from the door and spun around. Pickle had her front paws on the first step of the grand staircase. Sal, poised on her back, looked worried. "We're not going upstairs, are we?" he squeaked.

"Yes, we are," said Pickle before Toby could answer. "We may not have meant to come here, but seeing as we are, we ought to take a good look around. This is the closest we've come to finding out anything about Candy."

Toby couldn't dispute this. He hadn't been about to suggest they leave anyway. He nodded, took a breath, glanced warily up the stairs and joined Pickle. "I'll go first," he whispered and began to climb.

The staircase seemed more solid than he'd expected, given the general state of everything else, but even so, there were enough groans and creaks in the first few steps to give Toby pause. He side-stepped closer to the balustrade, where the joints were solid enough that the weight of the dogs would not put extra stress on the treads. The staircase curved around and back on itself, past a wall covered in dark, flocked paper, with a ridiculously large, lighter rectangle where a painting had once hung.

The first floor smelt musty, perhaps in large part thanks to a rich red carpet—now grimy with muck—that remained in place. Stains ran down the walls where water had seeped through from the floor above. The hallways, one on each side, were lined with doors, just as they had been below.

The dogs rested for a moment. Toby pricked up his ears. Nothing of interest on this floor. Not to the left. He turned his head to the right. A door at the very end of the hall was swinging open, revealing a baby's crib shrouded with a beautifully embroidered, sheer silver lace canopy. The golden light of a chandelier lit up the stitching so that fireflies might have danced for the infant's amusement. Fragrance drifted out towards Toby. Expensive perfume, something old-fashioned. Hairspray and white linen ... Toby started, nearly falling backwards down the stairs. Pickle caught him by the collar and set him straight. When Toby peered down towards the nursery once more, the crib, the canopy and the chandelier had disappeared.

The room was dead.

Toby breathed out heavily. "Should we explore some of the rooms?" he asked Pickle. He already knew what her answer would be, but the constant surprises were emotionally draining for him.

"I can't hear anything," Sal whispered. "Maybe there's nothing here at all. Maybe those men didn't actually come inside—"

"They're here." Pickle glowered at Toby. "Somewhere."

Toby padded across the carpet, turning left, lifting his nose to sniff. Yes. He could smell someone. More than one person, in fact. Definitely Ryan. He recognised his scent from earlier.

"Ah!" Pickle caught her breath. "I hear water. Listen."

A trickling. Then the wheeze of an old pipe.

From above.

Toby indicated they should go up again. Sal covered his eyes. "Why-oh-why-oh-why?" he lamented, but quietly, because he was as invested in remaining as quiet as the dogs.

The second floor smelt even more strongly of

damp. The ceilings had collapsed in a couple of places and the walls showed a lot of water damage. With no carpet here, the wooden floorboards squished beneath their feet. *Ewww.*

"I told you," said a voice, instantly recognisable as Lionel's.

Toby froze, his hackles rising, his shoulders tense.

"I know you did, but Lionel, I think it's too risky." That was Ryan.

"Pour the tea, little bro," Lionel ordered, his tone exasperated.

Pour the tea? Toby frowned. That sounded innocuous enough, like the two men weren't searching for a schnauzer-collie-whippet-terrier-thingie or a poodle carrying a rat on her back.

The direction of the voices told Toby they were up ahead. Two of the doors in the left hallway—or was it a wing, Toby didn't know how you'd refer to it—were ajar. Toby motioned to Pickle to stay where she was. Sal looked simultaneously relieved and horrified at the idea they were splitting up, so he dug his heels into Pickle's back and squeaked.

Too loud.

Toby cringed and directed them back onto the staircase, following them down and pressing himself into the wall—as though that would prevent anyone from spotting them.

"What was that?" Ryan asked.

"What was what?" Lionel replied, a might tetchily. "I didn't hear anything. This place is like a morgue. You're so jumpy, Ryan. I'm not sure you're cut out for this work."

"I absolutely agree with you," Ryan said and laughed. "I'm totally done with it!"

"Don't be daft!"

"I'm not being daft, Lionel. I'm telling you!" Something slammed, perhaps a fist on a piece of furniture.

"Steady on!"

"I love you, man. You're my big brother. You've always looked after me—"

"And I'm going to continue to do that—"

"What? In prison?" Now Ryan sounded tearful.

"Lay off, Ryan!"

"No!" Ryan was properly losing it now. "Prison is where we're going to end up—"

"Not if you keep your mouth shut!" There was something of a veiled threat in Lionel's tone.

Ryan began to sound defensive. "I do! I will! Whatever! I'd never drop you in it! You know me."

"I certainly thought I did, but now I'm not so sure." Lionel sounded thoughtful.

"I didn't sign up to murder anyone!" Ryan told him meekly.

Lionel jollied him along. "That was an accident, bro. You know that."

"Maybe."

"It was," Lionel replied firmly.

"You told me, back at the beginning, it would be a couple of weeks' work. You said we would be helping some old woman out with the restoration of this house. A bit of fetching and carrying. A bit of DIY ... and that would be it. We'd have a room—"

"We do have a room—"

"But look at the state of it, Lionel. It's not fit for human habitation. In fact, it's not fit to keep dogs in—"

"Although we have—"

"Exactly! Instead of painting and decorating, we've been involved in a murder and we've stolen three dogs!"

Three dogs. Pickle and Toby exchanged glances.

"Stay here," Toby whispered to Pickle. "I'm going to try to get a look."

"Be careful," Pickle whispered back.

Sal clutched his heart and keeled over.

Toby arched his neck forward until his snout edged out around the corner. He sniffed. He could smell sweat. Cigarettes. Chicken flavour crisps. Tea. And ... digestive biscuits. *Ooh.* The brothers were taking a tea break? How remarkably civilised.

He slid along the hallway, pressing into the wall, ears and nose straining.

"Now she wants us to grab another one," Ryan grumbled.

"She likes dogs. What can I tell you?" Lionel sounded muffled, as though he were munching on a biscuit.

"So do their owners," Ryan replied tartly. "That's what I can't quite get my head around. It's so mean, nicking people's dogs! Why doesn't she rescue a couple instead?"

"She wants awards and prizes and stuff," Lionel said. "She won't get that from a bunch of traumatised mongrels!"

Excuse me, thought Toby and wiggled his eyebrows. *I'm a show dog!*

"So you draw the line at stealing dogs, but murder's okay?" Lionel asked.

"No! Quite clearly I said it isn't." Ryan was becoming frustrated. "I'm telling you, I don't want to do any of this. I want out."

Toby had reached the edge of the door. He couldn't tell by sound and scent alone whether either of the men inside were looking towards the open door. Presumably they were facing each other—either they were facing east and west, or they were facing north and south. It gave him a fifty-fifty chance of not being seen.

"Pour the tea, Ryan."

Toby hunkered down and slid forward on his belly. Only an inch. He could hear the chink of a teapot. This made for better odds because one or both of them would now be distracted. It was now or never. He slunk forward until he could see. The men were standing in the corner of the room, both young, both with sandy-blond hair, although one had a neatly clipped goatee, both wearing dark suits and smart shirts and ties. The one with the goatee wore pointed shoes made of what might have been crocodile hide—they had that kind of texture. The other had on a pair of worn black boots. Together, they looked like gangsters, which was outlandishly out of place in a run-down mansion house in East Devon, but still. The room itself was some kind of bedsit, with a mini kitchen in one corner and a sunken sofa and a battered armchair arranged around a beaten-up coffee table. There was a small square dining table, badly scratched, and a television resting on its box against the wall. The room, as Ryan had pointed out, wasn't remotely habitable, and a quick look at the badly stained mugs in the kitchen area confirmed Toby's initial impression. The stylish suits appeared incongruous in such surroundings.

With the men's attention on their tea and biscuits, Toby rose smoothly to his feet and swept past the open door and onto the next one. This room was empty. No sign of the old woman the brothers kept talking about. However, it had been recently inhabited. There were blankets on the floor. Toby crept in, one ear on the conversation next door, the other straining to listen for any unusual noises coming from elsewhere.

"I tell you what," Lionel was saying. "Let's do this one last job together tomorrow, and then you and I can go our separate ways."

"I told you, Lionel. I'm not up for stealing any more dogs."

Toby frowned. This would be the golden retriever they were discussing.

"I can't do this alone, bro. I need you. Any dog show worth its salt is going to have shedloads of security. How am I supposed to steal a prize-winning dog from under the owner's nose by myself?"

"Lionel—"

"*She'll* be there. She'll be angry if you don't show —" *The old woman?*

"I don't care."

"Well, you should care, Ryan!" Lionel's tone had turned ferocious. "Trust me! You won't like her when she's angry!"

"I don't like her anyway! I don't like what she wants us to do!"

There was a loud slap. A cry. "Ow!"

A scuffle. Boots on the floor. An upset mug.

"Ryan! Ryan! Pack it in!"

"You hit me!"

"I slapped you. It wasn't a hard slap. You need to calm down."

"You've never hit me before, Lionel!" Ryan sounded mournful, as though he were about to cry.

"I've never needed to." Lionel sounded broken, too. "I'm sorry, Ryan. I am. I'm sorry. But I need you. One last job. She's exhibiting one of the dogs and she wants us to grab another one. I can't handle two dogs on my own."

Toby glared through the wall. There you had it. Admission upon admission. The old woman—whoever she was—was paying these two goons to do her dirty work. Grabbing show dogs and exhibiting them as though they were her own.

And sanctioning murder.

Toby sniffed around at the blankets on the floor, working his way further into the room. He could smell … dried dog food. Treats. A definite doggy smell on the blankets, too. In the corner he found a small cage and a big silver bowl filled with slightly stale water. There had been at least one dog in here, possibly more. But where were they now?

If Lionel and Ryan were taking a dog to a dog show tomorrow, where were they keeping the dogs in the meantime?

"I can't. I'm sorry." Heavy footsteps across the floorboards. Toby realised with horror that Ryan was about to leave.

"Ryan!"

"Just leave me be, Li—" Ryan didn't get to finish. He was cut off by a smacking sound, followed by an almighty thud. The floor vibrated beneath Toby's feet.

Silence.

Toby held his breath.

"Oh," Lionel said. "Oh my god." Something in his voice was heart-stoppingly bleak. "Ryan? Ryan?" A scrambling sound. "Ryan? Wake up, man!"

Curious, Toby tiptoed back to the door and peered out. All he could see was a pair of feet, toes pointing up. They didn't move.

"Ryan?" Lionel was crying.

Oh dear, thought Toby. He edged out a little further and sniffed at the boots. They smelled strongly of shoe polish with a hint of straw and ... horse droppings ... Hmmm. Interesting. He continued sniffing and glanced up, staring straight into the eyes of the young man with the bearded face, kneeling on the floor, cradling his brother's head in his arms.

"Where did you come from?" Definitely Lionel.

"Hi," said Toby. "Pleased to meet you." He hoped his voice would carry enough to alert Pickle to his predicament.

"You're not one of hers." Lionel sounded confused.

"I'm visiting," said Toby.

Lionel lay his brother's head down. Ryan groaned.

"Huh! You're alive?" Lionel slapped his brother's face.

Grimacing, Toby began to creep past Ryan's boots, but Lionel turned to him, quick as a flash, leaning forward and grabbing his collar.

Dang collar! thought Toby. *How many times have I told Clarissa that it's a liability?*

"She might like you," Lionel said, doing his best to inspect a wriggling Toby. "What are you? A schnauzer?"

"Trust me, she won't like me," Toby told him and, angling himself with difficulty, tried to bite Lionel's hand. When that didn't work, and Lionel only held him a little further away, pushing down on his neck with a cruel amount of force, Toby was forced to do something he'd never tried before.

Concentrating all his intent around his neck—particularly his collar—he cried, "*Scintilla*!" The resulting shock of energy knocked Lionel backwards. He let go of Toby's collar just as Ryan blinked and raised a hand to his head.

"What happened?" he asked, staring at Toby with bewilderment. "Who are you?"

"I'm Toby," said Toby. "But I can't stay and chat, I'm afraid. Bye!"

He skipped out into the hallway. "Pickle!" he barked. "Run!"

He scampered after her just as Lionel rushed out of the bedsit. "Get back here!" he roared, with no obvious awareness of basic dog training. Toby sprinted along the hall in the direction of the stairs.

He took them two by two, jumping down the last four without his paws touching the ground. It was a hard landing and, as he paused to recover and gather his breath, confident Lionel was never going to catch him and that Ryan was in no fit state to do anything, he glanced to his right, towards the nursery.

A woman floated away from him, heading for the nursery. Tall, slim. As she turned to close the door, she smiled at him, her eyes a bright shining silver. Toby recoiled in horror, blinked, and the door closed.

Lionel had made it to the stairs.

With no time to waste, Toby scarpered. He pelted down the next flight of stairs and into the hall, where the front door remained open. Diving through it, he tripped on the uneven paving and rolled against one of the vast stone urns.

"Urgh!" The impact took his breath away, but he couldn't take the time he needed to recover. He scrambled to his feet once more, a sharp pain emanating from the ribs on his right side, and chased along the rough stone path and down the hill, past the barn and the Mercedes, heading down the lane in pursuit of Pickle's furry back end, Sal's diminutive form bouncing around on top of her like a rodeo star. All he needed was a rhinestone cowboy outfit.

Catching up with Pickle, Toby matched her

stride for stride as they chased along to the end of the lane and out onto the main road. Pausing to catch their breath, Pickle stared in panic up the way they'd just come. "The car is moving!"

"The Merc?" Toby asked, moving closer to her so he could see. *Yep*. "We have to hide," he said.

"Where?" Pickle demanded. It was just their luck that this stretch of road had an open vista.

"Down there! In the hedge!" Toby said, indicating a patch of green bush about two hundred yards away. Once again they sprinted as though their lives depended on it, oblivious to the vehicles trundling and bumping past them.

"This is the sparsest hedge I've ever seen!" complained Pickle, throwing herself under a clump of bramble.

Toby thought of his friend Mad Mabel. "You need to make like a hedge," he said. "Become one with the hedge. No-one will ever see us then."

CHAPTER TWENTY-FOUR

By the time they arrived home, it was dark. They were exhausted from the long walk, hungry and—it goes without saying—filthy.

Toby, without thinking, led them through the dog flap and into the kitchen. He stared at his bowl. Empty.

"Toby?" Clarissa called. "Is that you?"

"It is!" he called back. "Hi!"

"Where have you been?" Clarissa called, her chair dragging on the floor as she extracted herself from the sanctity of her computer. "I've been worried si—eeeeeeeeeek!"

Toby jumped in alarm, whirling around, fearful that Lionel and Ryan had followed them. "What? Who's there?"

"Is that a *rat*?" Clarissa shrieked. "Get it out of here!"

"It's Sal," said Toby.

"Get. It. Out!"

"He's not going to hurt you," Toby protested.

"I know he's not going to hurt me because I'm going to exterminate him with one zap of my wand if he doesn't leave!"

Toby pouted. "Clarissa! That's not polite! Can I just explain?"

"It's fine," said Sal. "I get it." He slid off Pickle's back, his shoulders slumped. "Hoomans hate rats. Ain't nothing I can do about that. I'll go back to the shed. Pom's waiting for me, anyway."

Clarissa narrowed her eyes. "Is he *talking* to you?"

"Of course," said Toby. "Everyone talks to me."

"What's he saying?"

"Pretty much what you'd expect. Nobody loves me, everybody hates me—"

Clarissa angled her head. "Is he *with* you?"

Toby peered around the kitchen. There was nobody else present. "He's with me *and* Pickle," he said, slowly, in case Clarissa had suddenly become hard of understanding.

Sal slunk towards the door, chin on his chest, the

sorriest specimen that had ever had cause to enter—and exit—the house.

"Oh, for goodness sake," Clarissa huffed. "I suppose if he's *with* you, he can stay."

"He's with us, for better or worse," agreed Pickle.

Clarissa turned her attention to Pickle. "Why are you that colour?" she asked.

"What colour?" Pickle hadn't had time to think about her appearance for hours. Her paws hurt from the long walk, and she was famished and exhausted—and those were almost the only things she cared about. The fact that they hadn't been able to locate Candy was still at the forefront of her mind, of course, but for now she needed something to eat and some sleep.

"Why is Pickle grey? Dark grey!"

"Well ..." Toby began, but Clarissa was turning her attention to him.

Wrinkling her nose, she ran her fingers through Toby's fur. "Ugh. You're covered in dust!"

"It doesn't surprise me," said Toby. "We've had quite the adventure—"

"You've been down to that funeral home you were on about, haven't you? I told you to wait for me!"

"We started off at the funeral home," Toby

admitted, "but we ended up way out of town. Way, way, way out!"

"Toby!"

"I know, I know." Toby offered Clarissa his best you-know-me-I-just-can't-help-myself-but-please-love-me-anyway expression.

Clarissa pointed at the ceiling.

"Why don't you come up to the bath with me and tell me all about it?"

"I don't need a barf!" Toby protested. "Just a sammich and some sleep!"

"Up!" Clarissa stamped her foot.

"It's not fair," grumbled Toby.

Pickle laughed.

Clarissa surveyed the poodle once more. "And you, missy! Upstairs."

"I bet you don't even know how to give proper spa treatments," Pickle complained.

Clarissa nodded at Toby. "And bring your rat friend with you."

Clarissa chose to put both dogs in the tub together, but Sal, who would have been way out of his depth in the water, remained on the side with a chunk of sponge that Clarissa had broken off for him. He scrubbed at his armpits and chest with a surprising amount of glee. It turned out he'd never had a bath in warm water before and had never been introduced to soap and the resulting bubbles.

"I used to watch you guys in the salon all the time," he said. "It kinda looked fun, but I never had the opportunity to have a go."

"It's the best thing ever," said Pickle.

Toby wasn't inclined to agree, but he kept quiet because it would be rude to contradict.

Besides which, Clarissa was taking the opportunity to sound him out further about his day, and, between gagging on a mouthful of bubbles and answering Clarissa's questions, Toby was having trouble keeping up with Sal and Pickle's conversation.

"You hid in a coffin?" Clarissa couldn't quite believe what she was hearing.

"It was a spur-of-the-moment thing," said Toby, spitting bubbles.

"So you spent all this time closed up in a coffin?"

She really wasn't getting it at all.

"No, I told you. We were loaded into the back of a van and driven away—"

"Okay, but—"

"Then we managed to get free with a little of the old hocus-pocus." Toby waved a soapy paw at her, spattering her t-shirt with bathwater.

"Hold still, you terror!"

"And then we went off to explore the house." He stopped. What would Clarissa make of the strange visions he'd experienced? Like mirages from history.

"What?" Instinctively, Clarissa knew he was holding back. She scrubbed his head extra hard.

"Ow! We ... er ..." He decided not to tell her. Not immediately. Not until he'd had a chance to think about it all a little more. "We explored the house, and we found the two men that had arrived at the funeral director's place. We heard them admit to taking Candy and killing Pea's sister!"

Clarissa stopped scrubbing. The soap slipped down Toby's forehead and covered his snout. He sneezed.

"You heard the two men admitting to murder?"

"Yes." Toby sneezed again.

Clarissa reached for a towel and dried her hands. "We need to tell Ed."

"But there's more—"

"But he's going to want details. How am I going to explain that you overheard it and not me?"

Clarissa threw the towel back over her shoulder. “He’s never going to buy that.”

“He might,” said Toby. “It’s not like he doesn’t have his suspicions about us, I’m sure.”

“Can you identify these men?”

Toby recalled the goatee beard and the close-cut sandy hair. “Probably,” he said. “Especially the younger one because he’s going to have the biggest egg on his forehead tomorrow.”

“’Probably’ probably isn’t good enough.” Clarissa chewed on her finger. “Did you get the number plate?”

“Of the van? No.”

“Or the Merc?”

“No.” Toby shrugged. “Sorry. I should have.”

“Ugh.” Clarissa slumped down on the bathroom floor, wincing when she realised how sodden it was and how wet the back of her jeans had become. “There must be something we can use to persuade Ed that we’re onto something.” Her eyes lost focus for a moment as she thought back over the past few days.

She shook her head. “Let’s grab some supper and you can tell me everything all over again. I think you’ll need to start from”—she curled her lip—“the rats, and then take me through today.”

"Suppertime! Everybody out!" Toby ordered and, simultaneously, he and Pickle jumped out of the bath.

"Waaaaaaaaah!" Clarissa shrieked as they showered her with water. "Steady! One at a time!" But the horse had bolted ... or rather, the dogs had been set loose.

She covered each of them with a towel, then reached for another to offer Sal. As she went to hand it over, she realised he would drown in its folds. Looking around for something smaller, she settled on a facecloth hanging over the radiator.

"Here you are," she said, offering it to him. "It'll help you look less like a drowned rat."

"Ho ho," said Sal, and sniffed his fragrant armpits. "Coo! I smell gorgeous!"

CHAPTER TWENTY-FIVE

"Do you mind if we invite Pom in?" Toby politely asked Clarissa once they were downstairs. It always paid to stay on the same side as her, so even though Sal had already skipped out to the wizard shack to find his friend, Toby decided he'd pretend to ask Clarissa's permission.

"Who's Pom?" Clarissa asked, dividing up a tin of dog food between two bowls.

"Erm—" Sal and Pom entered through the dog flap, Pom's eyes wide with a mixture of fear and curiosity. This was a proper house, quite unlike the salon, and he'd never seen anything like it. "This is Pom," Toby announced.

Clarissa glanced over and squealed. "It's another rat!"

"He," said Toby. "Not *it*."

"How many more are there?"

"None as far as we know," Toby reassured her.

"As far as you know? What kind of an answer is that? I don't want my kitchen overrun with the little —" Clarissa caught her breath. Sal and Pom stood together, staring up at her with sweet black eyes. Fat Sal, still damp from his bath, and skinny Pom. They seemed tiny in comparison with the dogs. Clarissa bit back her words. "Alright. Ugh. What do rats eat?"

Toby stared doubtfully at Sal. "I think they eat everything ..."

"Given half the chance," Sal agreed.

"Cheese and chocolate biscuits, in my experience," said Pickle.

"You can't go wrong with cheese and biscuits," Sal agreed.

"Cheese and biscuits," Toby dutifully relayed.

"That doesn't seem like a particularly healthy diet to me," Clarissa noted.

Sal pointed at the vegetable basket. "We like carrots."

"Carrots," Toby added.

"I'll fix them something," Clarissa agreed, and swiftly delivered two bowls of dog food to Pickle and Toby and two small saucers of carrot mixed with dog biscuits and some cheese scrapings for Sal and Pom. For her part, she settled on a cheese sandwich.

Toby eyed it jealously and decided he'd better sit next to her while telling his story.

He did so, snuggled on the sofa alongside his favourite hooman, relaying all of his recent adventures with Pickle, Sal and Pom. Pickle curled up in Toby's basket, trying to keep her eyes open. Sal and Pom perched politely on the edge of the hearth, their long tails wrapped around themselves. Once Toby had finished, Clarissa stood up and split her sammich corners between all of the animals—much to Toby's consternation—before grabbing her laptop and returning to the sofa.

"I think there's a few things worth thinking about here," she said, flipping up the lid and activating the screen. "I'm going to find it hard to explain to Ed how I know that these men—Lionel and Ryan, was it?"

Toby nodded.

"—are involved. If we could find out a little more about them ..." She began hitting keys. "Like, maybe ... Hmmm. Does Carnation Funeral Director's have a website?" She shuffled through the results her search had thrown up and shook her head. "No. Let's try something else. Erm …" More tippity-tapping. "Here!"

Toby leaned closer to take a look.

"See?" She showed him. "This is information from Companies House. Carnation's went out of business in … 1998. Wow."

"How come they still have vehicles, then?" Toby asked. "I mean, yeah, the place was all closed up and musty and stuff—"

"And the hearse had flat tyres," Pickle remembered.

"That's true," said Toby. "It can't have been used for a really long time."

"Maybe someone has bought the warehouse?" Clarissa did another search. "Hmm. It last changed hands in 2002. Nothing since then. Weird to buy a place and not use it for over twenty years."

"Who bought it?" Toby asked, thinking of the woman with the odd eyes he'd seen in the country house. He assumed she must be the 'she' that Lionel and Ryan had been referring to.

"I can't find that level of detail," Clarissa said. "Unless it's on the election register, but I think that's unlikely."

She brought up Google Maps. "So, what about this house you visited?"

"It wasn't really a visit," Sal chipped in. "We were ratnapped."

"Dognapped," Pickle corrected him.

"Dognapped? Not at all. All part of my great plan," Toby muttered.

Clarissa snorted. "Yeah, right." She angled the laptop to give him a better view. "Describe which way you came back. Bushy Leaze?"

Bushy Leaze would take him up to Sparky's house. "No," he decided, thinking about the turns and the straight runs. "It's on the road we would take if we were going to see Mabel."

"Towards Lyme Regis? Right." Clarissa honed in on the road and clicked on satellite view. Using two fingers, she manipulated the screen to focus in or draw out. "Looks like there's a couple of likely properties ... but I can't tell much about them *virtually*. We'd have to go and visit them."

"We can't do that yet!" Pickle said. "Our first priority is the dog show."

Toby nodded wryly. "I agree with Pickle. She says the priority has to be the dog show."

Clarissa scrunched her face up. "Hmm. I know you mentioned something about a dog show ... but ... what do you mean by it's your priority?"

"Well, we'll be going along to it tomorrow," Toby told her. "Obvs."

"Obvs?" Clarissa raised her eyebrows. "Where is it?"

"Check on the thingummy," Toby said, waving a paw at the laptop.

Clarissa typed in the words dog, show and Sun Valley. "Mmm. There's one in ... Seatown and one in ... oh, no ... that's Saturday. There aren't many on tomorrow at all. I suppose most shows are held at the weekend." She clicked on the link to the Seatown one. "Oh. No. This one happened in 2020. I think you must be mistaken about what you heard, Toby."

"Do the search again but without Sun Valley," Toby suggested.

Clarissa did so. "Whoa." She sat back and laughed. "Yes. There is a dog show tomorrow. And some dog show it is, too!"

Toby peered over her shoulder. "Fluffts?" he read.

"Only one of the biggest, most prestigious dog shows in the world!" Clarissa told him.

"Then it must be that one!" Pickle barked with excitement. "That would make sense. They may be showing Candy there, and at the same time they're planning to steal a golden retriever."

"We should get an early night so we can be up bright and breezy," Toby suggested.

"Wait a minute!" Clarissa stalled him. "It's in Birmingham."

"Where-ee-uhm?" Toby asked.

"Birmingham."

"Soooooo?" Toby shrugged. British geography was not his strong point. "Is that a problem?"

"It's about three hours up the motorway!"

Pickle stood up and shook herself. "We'll definitely need to make an early start, then. I'm going to enjoy my final ablutions and call it a night."

"Good idea." Toby slid off the sofa. "I'll join you."

"Hang on—" Clarissa tried to intervene.

"I'll tuck Sal and Pom in the shed too," Toby added.

"You're not listening to me!" Clarissa raised her voice. "I can't just take a day off work to shepherd you lot around the country, you know."

"Of course you can!" Toby told her. "This could be a *huge* story for you!"

Pickle padded towards the kitchen. "Not to mention it's a matter of life and death."

"If you don't take us, how will we get there?"

Toby asked, joining Pickle at the threshold to the kitchen.

Clarissa opened her mouth to protest, thought better of it and clamped her lips together.

"Exactly," said Toby.

Clarissa pushed herself from the sofa. "I don't think you're thinking this through properly. All the evidence points to the fact that these men are extremely dangerous. They killed Hyacinth, after all."

"Terribly dangerous men," said Sal. "Big fists. Angry voices."

"Lionel claimed killing Hyacinth was a mistake," Toby said.

"He was lying," Pickle growled.

"I'm afraid I agree with Pickle." Pom spoke up for the first time, his voice quivering as he looked from Pickle to Clarissa and on to Toby. "From what I saw, it was a deliberate act of harm."

"We'd best stay home," Sal said, not that anyone was listening to him.

Clarissa's head swivelled between the animals as they conversed, waiting for Toby to translate.

Toby rolled his eyes. "Guys! Guys! Alright, they're dangerous. But that's no reason *not* to go after them."

"I'd say it was all the more reason *to* go!" Pickle stamped a paw. "We have to put a stop to what they're doing—"

"And save a golden retriever!" Toby added.

"And if there's any chance—any chance at all—that we can find Candy, then surely we have to take it?" Pickle pleaded.

"That too!" Toby stared up at Clarissa. "We have to find Candy. I gave my word."

"Alright. Alright." Clarissa sighed. "The thing is, it's Ed's day off tomorrow. We were planning to spend the day together."

"Invite him along!" Toby breezed. "It'll be a lovely day out!"

"Ha!" Clarissa closed her eyes. "Of course it will."

"And ask him to drive," Toby added as an afterthought. "We're more likely to get there in one piece."

CHAPTER TWENTY-SIX

"Are we there yet?" Toby asked for the umpteenth time.

"We're not even at Gloucester yet!" Clarissa, in the passenger seat, turned her head to give him 'the look'.

"Does he need a wee?" Ed asked. "Is that why he's creating?"

"I'm not creating," Toby contradicted. "Although I am, indeed, creative. Thank you for noticing."

"Toby!" Clarissa hushed him.

"I could do with a strong coffee and a bacon sarnie, anyway, so maybe we'll call in at the next services," said Ed, stifling a yawn. It had been an early start for him after a run of long shifts.

"Bacon sammich! Now you're talking." Toby

settled happily back into his seat beside Pickle. "Please may I have brown sauce on mine?"

"I'm not buying you one," Clarissa said, facing the front again.

"It's okay," Ed said, looking sideways at her. "I brought my wallet. They're on me."

Clarissa flushed.

"How far until the next services?" Toby asked.

"A few miles."

Ed laughed. "I could swear you're talking to each other."

Clarissa faked a giggle. "What do you think he'd say if he could talk?"

"I think he'd be asking you for a bacon sandwich."

"Yeah, he'd love one."

"I really would," said Toby. "So open your wallet, let the moths fly free, Ed, and get your money out."

"Those rats you've brought along?" Ed asked.

"Yes." Clarissa grimaced.

"Are they your new pets?"

Clarissa hesitated. "Kind of."

"Mm-hmm." Ed indicated and pulled out to overtake another vehicle. "They're not shredding my back seat, are they?"

"No, no. Don't worry. They're asleep."

Truth to tell, Sal had his eyes closed and was curled up in a tight ball because of his nausea. The whole travelling in a car thing really wasn't for him. Every now and then he would emit a little moan.

"It would probably be best to pull over sooner rather than later," Toby suggested. "I think Sal needs to nibble a little grass. Are we nearly there?"

Clarissa reached forward and turned the music up.

"I think she's trying to drown me out," Toby said.

Sal moaned again. "I can't think why," he said.

Clarissa cleared her throat.

The services were a long way behind them now, and they'd waved at Gloucester as they passed by. Traffic was heavier the closer to Birmingham they drove, but they'd made good progress and would be at the show for ten as planned.

"There's something I need to tell you," she said to Ed.

Toby perked his ears up.

"Alright." Ed cast a glance her way. "You're not going to tell me we're finished already, are you?"

"No! Don't be silly!" She reached out and squeezed his knee. Toby watched her. She should be using that hand to scruggle his ears, not Ed's knee!

"You're not seeing someone else?"

"No."

"Okay." Ed breathed deeply. "Wait! Are you married?"

"Ed!" Clarissa guffawed. "Will you stop?"

"That's a relief," said Ed. "Fine. Go on. I can take anything."

"It's about why we're attending this dog show."

"I thought you wanted to because of Pickle? That's what you said last night on the phone." Ed sounded confused. "I know you're not showing her, but—"

"No, but that's partly it." Clarissa hesitated. "We —I mean I—well, we—Oh! This is hard."

"Just tell him I'm the superbrain behind all this," Toby chipped in, striving to be helpful.

"*I!*" reiterated Clarissa, loudly. "I have a feeling that the men who murdered Hyacinth will be at Fluffts today."

"You have a *feeling*?" Ed asked, concentrating on the road.

"Yes. I think you should arrest them."

"Hold on," Ed laughed. "Why do you have a

feeling? I can't arrest someone just because you have a feeling. I need hard evidence."

"Like what?" Clarissa asked. "Couldn't you arrest them and then, I don't know, search their vehicles or premises or something afterwards?"

"It doesn't work like that. I'd have to get a warrant to do any searches, which means I have to have probable cause—and again, that requires hard evidence."

"Oh." Clarissa huffed and stared out of the passenger window at the increasingly industrial landscape.

"Tell him about the dognapping," Toby suggested.

Clarissa pulled on her seatbelt, loosening the tension. "These men are dognappers," she told Ed. "That's why I think they'll be at Fluffts today. They're planning to steal a golden retriever."

"How do you know this?"

Clarissa smiled. "I'm a journalist. You know I can't reveal my sources."

"Hmmm." Ed pursed his lips, thinking. "You'll be able to identify them, though?"

Clarissa glanced at Toby. Toby looked at Pickle. Pickle exchanged glances with Sal. Sal nodded knowingly at Pom.

"Yes," squeaked Pom.

"Yes," said Sal.

"Yes," said Pickle.

"Absolutely," said Toby.

"We will," Clarissa told Ed.

"Alright then. When we get to the arena, I'll have a chat with security and circulate a description of these men."

"Great!" said Clarissa, and pointed out the turning to the National Exhibition Centre.

Ed indicated and moved onto the slip road. "Then we'll hang out with the golden retrievers and see what happens."

"You'll probably get wagged to death," said Toby. "Those goldies are always so darn happy."

"Exhaustingly so," agreed Pickle. "I get a migraine whenever one comes to the salon."

"Any chance of another sammich before we go in?" Toby asked. "You know, like brain food?"

"Absolutely not," said Clarissa.

"No? You don't like golden retrievers?" Ed asked, assuming she was talking to him.

Clarissa put her head in her hands. "Why is my life so complicated?" she asked.

But nobody had an answer to that.

CHAPTER TWENTY-SEVEN

"Welcome to Fluffts!"

Toby had never seen so many dogs in one place before. The NEC was heaving with people—some in uniform, most in some form of countryside or walking garb—and dogs of every shape and size. Curly tails, straight tails, fluffy tails, no tails. Little legs, lanky legs, strong legs, fluffy legs and tri-paws! Dogs in every one of the colours that nature created them, with ears that pricked and perked or twitched or lay flat, noses that sniffed out every secret within a mile radius, and shiny, intelligent eyes that didn't miss a trick.

"Wow," said Ed. "I didn't know there were this many dogs in the world!"

Toby blinked. Surely Ed was kidding? This was the tip of the iceberg!

Ed reached down and stroked Toby's head. "You're just as handsome as any of them, mate!"

Toby wagged. "Thanks, Ed. Obviously, I agree."

"There's the security office." Ed pointed it out. "I'll go and have a chat. You head over to the golden retrievers and I'll catch up with you."

"Rightio," said Clarissa, taking Toby's lead from him. She was already juggling Pickle and the rats—both of whom were riding inside her backpack, with their little heads poking out to stare at their surroundings. Toby doubted there were many rats in the UK who had travelled as far as this pair.

"I'll bring more coffee," said Ed. "I need another fix."

He sailed away as Clarissa checked a handy map for directions to the golden retrievers. "I'm going to end up over-caffeinated if I keep drinking as much coffee as Ed. He's far too grown-up. I'd prefer a bottle of fizzy pop." She ran her finger over the map. "Gundogs. That would be them. We need to go down here and over the bridge." She clucked her tongue like a mother hen. "Walk nicely, you two."

They set off, tails waving, noses engaged. *So many exciting sniffs! Ooh! A pupcake stall!*

Tony indicated the stall and Clarissa had a browse. Seeing the price, she choked. "How much? Goodness!"

Oh. Toby pulled a sad face. A little further on he spotted an ice cream stall. *Ohmydogness! Proper doggy ice cream!* But Clarissa pulled them away from that too. There were stalls and concessions with everything from collars and leads to toys, baths and paddling pools to beds and cages, kennels to fit any dog and even doggy hot tubs. Toby loitered in front of that concession far longer than he should have. Eventually Clarissa had to drag him away.

"You're mean," he told her.

Clarissa shook her head. "Babe, if you want a hot tub, all you have to do is fart in the bath. It'll save me a fortune."

"Vulgar," said Toby.

"You were doing it last night," Pickle pointed out.

"Yada, yada." Toby flounced ahead of them, not that he could get far, given he was attached to Clarissa. They climbed to the first floor and took the bridge that would lead them over to the gundog hall, pausing once they were halfway across to gaze down at the sea of people moving around underneath.

Clarissa had quizzed Toby on Lionel's and

Ryan's appearance and passed the descriptions on to Ed, but finding the men here—young and sandy-haired, one with a goatee—would not be easy. "This is going to be a needle in a haystack," Clarissa complained, resuming their trek to Hall 5. "Although, I suppose it'll be easier once we're with the golden retrievers. I hope so, anyway. Unless everyone here is heading that way."

"It looks like they are," moaned Pickle.

"They may be wearing suits," Toby suggested. "At least, they were yesterday."

"If they do, they'll stick out like a sore thumb," said Clarissa. "That would be really helpful!"

"And really stupid," said Pickle. "If I were them, I'd wear a disguise."

"What sort of disguise would dognappers wear?" Toby asked.

Clarissa pointed out a human in a Dalmatian suit walking towards them. "Maybe they'll dress up as a golden retriever!"

"Yoikes!" Pickle stopped to bark at the man in the dog suit. "Is that real Dalmatian skin?"

Toby guffawed. "No! It's a giant walking cuddly toy!"

Clarissa hastened to placate Pickle and wave at

the Dalmatian man as he continued on his way. "Hush!"

"It's not even a good likeness for a real Dalmatian," Toby tittered.

"And yet ..." Clarissa turned to watch the man disappear. "Hmmm. It's a thought. We'll need to be vigilant."

"We'll have to sniff every single person in a costume!" Toby agreed.

"Fun, fun, fun," said Clarissa. "Whatever you do, don't start ripping people's costumes off, okay? They may not be wearing much underneath—and I, for one, am not ready to see that."

The gundog area was as busy as Clarissa had expected. There were setters and pointers and springers and spaniels, vizslas, spinones and even Weimaraners. And, of course, retrievers in all their various flavours: curly coated, flat coated, Labrador and golden, and some Toby couldn't have named had he had an encyclopaedia of dog breeds in his paw.

Their owners, breeders, or those showing them worked hard at beautifying their prize pooches. There were portable grooming tables everywhere and the sound of hairdryers and clippers and sprays and brushes. Amazed by the perfect behaviour of the show dogs, Toby tried several times to start conversations with a few, but they either stared at him and Pickle in disdain or were too busy practising their moves to pay him any attention.

"Look at the state of me," Pickle lamented. "I don't know what Clarissa put in the bath last night, but my fur is almost yellow!"

"It isn't," Toby reassured her.

"It is! And what's more, she didn't brush me out properly, so now I've gone all super-curly!"

"I think you look pretty," Toby offered. He liked curls.

"And my nails are ruined. Ruined, I tell you!" Pickle lifted her nose and howled, startling a golden retriever to their right, who promptly fell off his grooming table.

"Steady," said Toby.

"I should be here!" Pickle cried, more melodramatic than Toby had seen her for a few days. "Well, not *here* exactly. Not *here* with these plebian breeds. No, I should be in the toy hall!"

"I'd love to be in the toy hall, too!" enthused Toby. "All those borlies and bears!"

"Not that kind of toy, you doofus!" Pickle sighed.

"The premier breeds! Come to that, we should be in the toy hall anyway. If the old woman is showing Candy, that's where they'll be."

"That's true!" Toby thought about it for a moment. "We'll tell Clarissa we need to go over there as soon as the golden retrievers have finished, okay?"

"Alright." Pickle sniffed disconsolately at a table leg.

"If we haven't spotted the Bruise Brothers by then, we've either missed them or we've come to the wrong show."

Clarissa wound her way around the tables, stopping occasionally to admire a particularly handsome and happy retriever and chatting to the owner, while Toby, Pickle and the rats kept their eyes peeled for anyone who looked vaguely familiar.

When Ed finally caught up with them, they found an area where they could sit together and take a load off while simultaneously watching everything going on around them.

"The security office was really helpful," Ed told Clarissa. "They're sending extra staff along to cover this area, so if anyone does try anything, there'll be plenty of hands to help out."

"People who steal dogs should get a long prison sentence," Clarissa said, thinking of poor Hyacinth.

She'd sacrificed her life to try and prevent someone from taking her beloved pet.

"It doesn't work like that though, does it," Ed told her. "Rightly or wrongly, and I do believe wrongly, dogs are classified as property, so cases are dealt with in the courts that way."

"Appalling," Clarissa told him. "So many pets are treasured members of the family. Even more so when people don't have children for whatever reason."

"I know," said Ed, and hugged her. "Don't worry. If these men make a move, we'll find them."

If I were stealing a dog, what would I wear? Toby wondered. Wearing a dog costume would surely call attention to yourself. *I can't see Lionel dressing up as a dog somehow,* he decided. *But he'd probably make Ryan do that ...*

He eased a crick in his neck. Faces were beginning to blur into one. *So many hoomans look exactly the same.* Toby hunkered down, staring out at all the legs moving past. The bedsit in the country house where the pair of them were staying had been sparse, suggesting they didn't have many belongings with them. That would make sense if they were staying there at the behest of the old woman.

In turn, that suggested it was unlikely there would be dog costumes.

Or many extra pairs of shoes.

Toby recalled the shiny shoes Lionel had been wearing. The pointy toe. The leather that might have been crocodile hide or something equally gross. With that in mind, he began to take a keen interest in footwear.

The golden retrievers entered the ring for the first time. Toby hadn't realised how many classes there would be for each breed. This event was totally different to a family dog show—more professional, more formal, more ... intense. He watched the dogs briefly, the heavy tails sweeping the air, the merry eyes and smiley faces, but given they all looked almost exactly alike, he soon lost interest and went back to shoe-watching.

Unfortunately, it soon transpired that watching the movement of legs is rather mesmerising. Toby became lost in a world of trainers and walking boots, or riding boots and wellies, of sensible shoes and flip-flops, of plastic soles and crêpe soles ... his head began to nod ... and pixie boots and ... as things began to blur ... crocodile uppers.

Toby sat up so fast he banged his head on Clarissa's elbow and knocked her coffee flying.

"Owwwwww!" she squawked, shaking spilt coffee from her hand and rubbing her damp jeans with the other. "Well done, Tobes! I'm going to stink of coffee all day now!"

"Do you have any tissues?" Ed asked, and Clarissa reached for her bag, accidentally knocking the rats off the top where they'd been happily sitting.

"I've seen him. I've seen Lionel!" Toby cried. "We have to arrest him!"

Clarissa forgot about the coffee and the spreading stain on her jeans. "Where?"

"What?" Ed asked, reaching for Pickle's lead because she too had become agitated.

"They're here!" Clarissa told him. "Somewhere. Toby—" She leaned down and unclipped Toby's lead.

Ed put out a hand to stop her. "What are you doing? You can't let him off. There are signs all over the place saying dogs must be kept on a lead at all times!"

Clarissa shook his hand away. "Toby is going to find them for us."

"But we can't do anything even if we see them," Ed reminded her, struggling to hold a wriggling Pickle. "They haven't done anything wrong." Pickle began barking.

"Yet." Clarissa nodded at Toby, who gazed up at her, waiting for permission. "Go!"

He darted away.

Pickle wrenched hard against Ed, almost pulling him off his feet. "Let me go!"

"Hey!"

Too late. Ed was forced to let go of her lead, and she scrambled after Toby.

"Come back!" yelled Ed, but they'd gone.

CHAPTER TWENTY-EIGHT

"Where did you see him?" Pickle panted as she caught up with Toby.

"He was coming this way, towards the grooming tables and the dog cages." He led her through a labyrinth of pet stations, each belonging to one show team.

"Did you see what he was wearing?"

"I only saw the shoes," Toby admitted. "But what are the odds? It must have been him, right?"

"Loose dog!" someone called. "Security?"

"Oh, blast!" Toby cast a little shade in the direction of the tattle-tale. "You need to keep an eye on your own dog," he grumbled, and slipped under one of the grooming tables before quickly darting to the next. Pickle followed quickly, putting some distance between themselves and the eagle-eyed supergrass.

When they figured they were far enough away, Toby lay on his stomach and peered under the tables, beginning to watch shoes again. Pickle joined him.

At first it seemed Toby might have been mistaken, but with each dog observing two sides, they were able to scan effectively. It was Pickle who spotted the footwear this time. "There!"

Toby scurried to her side and squinted through the tables. "Yes! Come on!"

Manoeuvring out of their hiding place, they dodged around hooman legs, dog legs and table legs until they could finally see their quarry. Initially, Toby thought they'd made a mistake; the man they were tailing, although the right height and build, had a red tinge to his hair. He was pushing some kind of trolley with poles sticking out of it. Puzzled, Toby kept his distance until the man parked the trolley and angled right to begin fussing a dog. This golden retriever—proudly displaying half a dozen rosettes and a cup with red ribbons tied to the handles—had been left in his cage by his owner. Once the man showed his profile, Toby could clearly see the goatee. This was Lionel alright. He'd washed his hair with some sort of dye by the look of it, but he hadn't bothered with the beard.

"That's just lazy," Toby muttered. "A schoolboy error, sir."

"No sign of the other one," Pickle said.

"Maybe he stood his ground and decided not to come." Toby examined Lionel's clothing. He was wearing utility trousers and a green sweatshirt with the yellow Fluffts logo on it. He also sported a lanyard.

Toby was familiar with lanyards. Clarissa had had occasion to wear one while she was working for the Ministry of Witches on the zombie project. They lent an air of officialdom to even the lowest-paid worker. Nobody would question someone wearing an official lanyard.

"I'll bet old Lionel here has never done an honest day's work in his life," Toby muttered. "He's nicked that off someone."

"That means there's a seriously unhappy worker around somewhere," Pickle observed.

Toby slunk a little closer to Lionel, standing a few feet away from the trolley. He could see now that the wooden poles belonged to a broom and a mop. The trolley carried bags and cleaning equipment on top with a cubbyhole underneath for further supplies. Loo roll, perhaps.

Lionel, muttering softly, leaned closer to the retriever. After checking no-one was watching, he slipped a halter over the dog's neck before hastily pulling it out of its cage. The dog came without fuss, used to being handled by strangers and not for a moment recognising the danger.

And that's where the trolley came into its own.

Lionel opened a side panel and encouraged the dog inside. Although reluctant, with a little encouragement, it climbed in. Lionel closed the door.

That was good enough for Toby. He began barking. "Stop, thief! Stop, thief!"

Lionel, alarmed by the imperative nature of Toby's bark, pivoted in surprise. Seeing Toby, his eyes widened. "You again?" he spat.

Pickle took up the cry. "Stop, thief!"

"Stop, thief!" Toby barked. "Stop—"

"Right you are, sunshine!" A hand reached over and grabbed him by the collar. "Who do you belong to, hey?"

Toby struggled in the stranger's grasp, trying to spin around to get a better look. A security guard.

"You've nabbed the wrong man!" Toby told him.

"Go after him. The pretend caretaker! He went that-a-way!"

"Calm down, fella. We'll pop you in a kennel—"

"Over my dead doggy body!" Toby retorted, preparing to unleash his fabulous electric shock spell.

The poor security guard was saved from a nasty jolt by the appearance of Clarissa and Ed, the rats hot on their heels. "It's okay, officer!" Clarissa called. "That's my dog. *Those* are my dogs—"

"Really, madam? You realise you are required to keep your dogs on a lead—"

"At all times. I know, I know!"

The security guard kept a firm grasp of Toby's collar. Pickle danced around the pair of them, apoplectic with rage. "I'm quite within my rights to ask you all to leave the NEC—"

Toby rolled his eyes. *See? Give a man a lanyard and he'll assume he can run the world and be the boss of everyone!* "Unhand me!" he barked. "I'm innocent."

"Are you paid to be an idiot?" Pickle demanded of the poor security guard. He backed away in the face of her anger but didn't relinquish his hold of Toby.

"This poodle is quite out of control!" he cried.

"Toby! Pickle!" Clarissa snatched at Pickle and tried to soothe her. "I'm really dreadfully sorry," she told the security guard.

"Don't be sorry!" growled Pickle. "The bad guy is getting away with another dog!"

"Lionel's getting away!" Toby yelped. "We have to stop him!"

Clarissa frowned as his words began to sink in. "You found him?"

"Yes!" Toby and Pickle bellowed at once.

"He's getting away!" said Pickle.

"He has a housekeeping trolley!" Toby added.

"They found him," Clarissa told Ed.

"Who?" Ed looked blank.

"The dog thief!" Clarissa reached forward and took Toby's collar from the security guard. "Thanks so much for looking after him. I'll take it from here."

The security guard refused to let go. "I'm sorry, madam, I'm going to have to ask you to accompany me to the main entrance."

There followed a short tug of war until Clarissa, realising how demeaning it was for both her and Toby, let go of Toby, leaned towards the security guard and sharply flicked him on the forehead with her forefinger. "Sleep!" she said, and the security guard collapsed in a heap on the floor.

The dogs quietened immediately.

Ed paled. "What did you do?" He clasped his hands to his head.

"Never you mind," Clarissa replied, irritated now. "We have to go after the dog thief."

"Come on!" Toby called, rallying the troops. "This way!"

"Oh dear." A woman crouched down next to the guard. "What happened?"

"He fainted. It's a little warm in here, don't you th—" Clarissa began to explain as she edged away, but at that moment Pom and Sal chose to make an appearance, climbing over the security guard's body in an attempt to catch up with Toby.

The woman squealed and shot backwards, tripping over her feet and knocking a portable grooming station sideways. It screeched, the legs wobbled and gave way. "Mouse!" she screamed over the racket. "Mice!"

A couple of other people who'd been attracted to all the drama began to back away.

Sal stopped where he was, on top of the sleeping security guard's chest. "We're actually rats."

The woman screamed again, and suddenly it was bedlam as everyone began fighting to go in different directions. Toby, Pickle, the rats and Clarissa wanted to go one way, most of the bystanders wanted to go in the opposite direction to them, and poor old Ed didn't have a clue what was happening.

As another grooming table collapsed, scattering an array of salon equipment all over the floor, as women screamed and men shouted, as the tannoy announced the winner of the retriever puppy class, as dogs barked and complete chaos erupted all around, Ed could only look on with an air of bewilderment and long for the days when police officers had carried whistles, and crooks would throw their hands in the air and say, "It's a fair cop, guv'nor!"

CHAPTER TWENTY-NINE

"Come on!" Clarissa grabbed Ed's arm and pulled him after Toby and Pickle. With the rats following close behind and people scattering out of their way, they chased out of Hall 5 and into a concourse where they regrouped, heads swivelling, searching for a man with a caretaker trolley.

"We've lost him!" wailed Pickle.

"No," said Toby. "We've temporarily misplaced him, that's all."

"If he has a trolley, it stands to reason that he stole it from somewhere," Ed said. "I'm not saying he'll be returning it—"

"He was wearing a lanyard!" Toby told Clarissa. "He must have stolen both together."

"He was wearing a lanyard," Clarissa repeated to

Ed. "If he stole both at once, there's a chance that an NEC employee has already reported the theft."

"Yes!" Ed spun, searching the concourse for an employee with a radio. He raced over to a woman near the lifts and whipped out his warrant card. "I don't have time to explain," he told her, as Clarissa hurried to join him, "but I need you to get on your radio and find out whether anyone has reported a stolen caretaker's cart and a lanyard."

The woman picked up her radio. "I can already tell you that's the case," she said. "One of the facilities crew was assaulted about forty minutes ago."

"Where?" Ed asked.

"The housekeeping room, near Hall 9. It's the closest exit to the staff car park."

"Bingo," said Ed. "Which direction is that?"

"The other side of Hall 1 and then four halls down."

"That's miles!" complained Clarissa.

"It is quite a way," the woman admitted.

"Come on." Ed, although not one hundred per cent sure what was going on, set out with determination.

With so many people between them and Hall 9, there was every possibility they would never catch up with Lionel. Toby scanned his surroundings. His eye fell upon something that looked rather like the golf buggies he'd seen in films.

"Wait!" Toby called Clarissa back. "Over here!"

Clarissa halted and turned back to him.

"Let's take this!" Toby cried.

"Are you crazy?" she asked, hurrying over to where he was clambering into the driving seat. "We can't steal this!"

"Of course we can."

"The keys aren't even in it," Clarissa pointed out.

"That's not going to stand in our way, is it?"

Clarissa took a second to think it over. The clock was ticking. "Shove over," she said.

"What's going on?" Ed asked. "I thought time was of the essence?"

"It is," said Clarissa, making her mind up. "Get in."

"What?" Ed took a step away as Pickle jumped into the back, rapidly followed by the nimble-footed rats.

"Get in!" Clarissa and Toby roared together.

"But—"

Clarissa pushed him into the rear and jumped in the front. With a quick waggle of her finger, the electric engine purred into life. "Let's go!" she yelled.

"Yeeha!" sang Toby.

"I really hate cars," grumbled Sal. "They move too fast. It's just not natural."

His worst fears, however, were not realised. The buggy lurched forward as Clarissa grappled with the controls. She quickly found that there wasn't a great deal of skill to driving the buggy and that it had a top speed of around ten miles an hour.

"Crikey," moaned Toby. "I could run faster than this."

"A one-legged caterpillar could run faster than this," Pickle agreed.

"I quite like it," said Sal. "It's a bit easier on the stomach."

"Hey!" Someone was yelling behind them. Toby hung out of the passenger side to take a look. A man with a bright yellow vest with ASSISTANCE written in big letters. "Come back with my wheelchairs!"

"Wheelchairs?" Toby queried.

Ed swivelled around in his seat. "Oops. We've got two wheelchairs in the boot here, Clarissa. We ought to go back!"

"Too late!" Clarissa called. "We're committed now."

"Committed?" Ed muttered. "I need committing!"

“He’s coming after us!” Toby cried, pointing out the neon man. Clarissa leaned over and hauled him back into the seat.

“We need to go faster!” yelled Pickle.

“Clarissa! Stop!” shouted Ed.

“No way!” Clarissa waggled a finger at the car’s console and giggled. “*Velocitas*!”

The buggy lurched forward once more, but this time it began to speed up.

“Woooooooooooo!” Toby hollered.

Sal hid his head in his hands. “Oh no.”

Pickle bounced on her seat. “Go, go, go!”

“Grim,” groaned Sal.

“Clarissa—”

“Buckle up, detective!” shouted Clarissa. “Beep-beep! Everyone out the way! Beep-beep!”

“Coming through!” yelled Toby, standing on his back legs and supporting himself with one paw on the buggy’s side strut, waving his other paw as though he was brandishing a cutlass.

The buggy ‘sped’—at about thirty miles an hour, we’re not talking warp speed here—down the long corridor to Hall 4. Despite the crowds milling around in the concourse here, Clarissa skilfully navigated through everyone. Confusingly, Hall 3 was not next door to Hall 4 and neither was Hall 2, and so they soon found themselves outside Hall 1 and in the main entrance, where numerous ticket collectors and yellow-vested assistance assistants regarded them with suspicion.

Clarissa didn't care. She kept on going, zooming around corners and 'beeping' at pedestrians, leaving the poor unsuspecting souls scattered to the four winds.

The Hall 9 concourse was the busiest by far and, judging by the number of Chihuahuas, pugs, Pekingese, shih-tzus and poodles milling around, Pickle had her wish and they'd found the toy dog show. The problem was, given the popularity of these breeds, this particular part of the show was choc-a-bloc with visitors, and Clarissa couldn't plough through them without causing some serious damage. She jumped on the brakes, dislodging Toby. With nothing at the front of the buggy to prevent it, he was ejected from his seat.

"I'm flying!" he yelled, not unhappily, as he was catapulted through the air in the direction of a rather solid-looking wall. As luck would have it, his weight altered his trajectory and he landed plump in the middle of a stall selling honking plush ducks for discerning doggies.

Honk! Honk! Honk!

"Wooo! That was so much fun!" Toby, buried beneath dozens of ducks, freed his head and grinned up at the hapless proprietor of the duck stall.

"I'm so sorry about that!" Clarissa had exited the buggy in a more conventional way and had hurried over to rescue Toby. "Nothing's damaged, is it?"

"I … I don't think so." The poor man shook his head.

"Come on, Toby," Clarissa hissed. "You can't lie around all day!"

"I'm coming!" Toby extricated himself with some difficulty, every fresh move resulting in a *honk, honk, honk,* until finally he had four paws on the ground once more.

Ed joined them, clutching a rat in each hand. Sal lay limp.

"Does anyone have any smelling salts?" Pom asked.

Pickle, with her nose to the floor, suddenly barked. "I can smell Lionel!"

Clarissa rounded on her. "Do you have something?"

"This way!" Pickle, Toby rushing to join her, hurried forwards into Hall 9 and stopped next to a caretaker's trolley. "Here!"

"This one?" Clarissa asked doubtfully.

"It could be anyone's," Ed said. "There's more than one caretaker's trolley at an event this size."

"Well, *der*!" Toby rolled his eyes. "It smells of Lionel. I mean it absolutely reeks of him! You come and have a sniff, Detective!"

Pickle scratched at the storage area at the bottom of the trolley. "Open this!" she urged.

Clarissa quickly knelt and pulled the door open, fully expecting to see dozens of toilet rolls. "It's empty," she said.

Toby pushed alongside her so that he too could peer inside. "It's not completely empty," he noted.

"You're right," Clarissa said, reaching into the space and scooping up some hair. She pulled it out and examined it under the light, the tell-tale red, gold and white of a golden retriever.

"We must have just missed him," said Ed. "He's somewhere in this hall." Peering around, he spotted the welcome sight of a security guard's uniform and hurried to catch her. As Clarissa, Toby and Pickle watched from their position next to the caretaker's trolley, Ed spoke to the security guard, trying to gesture with his hands at the trolley and only then realising that he was still carrying the rats.

The security guard quirked an eyebrow but, when Ed handed her Pom to hold and fished out his warrant card, she nodded and reached for her radio. Ed accepted Pom back from her and rushed back to Clarissa and the dogs.

"For heaven's sake, Clarissa, can you look after these rats?" Ed asked, passing them over.

Sal opened his eyes briefly, then closed them again. Clarissa hurriedly dropped them into her rucksack, causing Sal to complain loudly from the depths of her bag where the dust of mints, used tissues and hand gel lived.

"The security guard is getting the office to check CCTV. She told me that there are doors at the rear of the hall which are used for loading and unloading. Maybe that's where he's headed," Ed suggested.

"Hurry! Hurry!" Clarissa, Toby and Pickle followed Ed as he rushed further into the hall. As in Hall 5, the show ring had pride of place in the centre, with a section for stalls and concessions, and a section for the grooming stations and dog cages, but here, more than in the previous hall, the stalls were three or four people deep, and the crowds made it impossible to see down the aisles.

Ed pulled up, Clarissa almost careering into him. Looking left and right, he made a quick decision and dived over the rope into the show ring. Toby, instinctively understanding what Ed was doing, leapt in after him and then jumped into his arms. There was a smattering of applause from the watching audience, despite the bewildered looks of the exhibitors in the ring and the glare from the judge.

Ed lifted Toby high. "Do you see him?" he asked.

"Hold still!" said Toby, sniffing the air. "Yes! Close!"

"Let him loose," Clarissa urged, and Ed placed Toby on the floor.

Toby sped away, barking. Pickle joined the chase, dashing through the ring and dodging legs, thoroughly enjoying the pandemonium, not something she would have believed only a few days previously.

And there was Lionel! Or rather, there were his crocodile shoes, strolling nonchalantly back the way they'd come, towards the entrance of Hall 9.

Why is he going that way? The thought crossed Toby's mind, but he was in too much of a hurry to care. He bore down on Lionel and, at the last moment, jumped and clamped his teeth on the bottom of Lionel's left trouser leg.

Lionel yelped and began to struggle, kicking his leg to try to dislodge Toby's grip. There were a couple of shouts of alarm from a few bystanders, but

Ed arrived within seconds and gripped Lionel's shoulder.

Lionel held his hands up to ward off a perceived assault. "Excuse me?" he said. "Take your hands off me!"

Ed brought out his warrant card once more. "DC Ed Plum, Devon and Cornwall Police. I have reason to believe you have taken a dog without the owner's consent."

"Where is it?" Clarissa, panting, joined them.

Lionel shrugged. "Do you see a dog, officer?"

And that was entirely the problem. Lionel was alone.

Ed glanced at Clarissa. She pulled a face, looking around desperately as security guards joined Ed.

"Sir?" one of them asked.

"We think this is the man who took the golden retriever from Hall 5," Ed told them.

"Where is it now?" the security guard asked.

"There's been some mistake," Lionel said. "I haven't taken any dog. I don't even like them." He snarled at Toby.

Toby snarled right back at him. "Why isn't he being arrested?" he demanded.

"They can't arrest him yet. They have nothing to arrest him for," Clarissa explained.

Pickle couldn't hide her outrage. "This is the man who killed Hyacinth! He has to be detained."

"As you can see, I'm just here doing my job." Lionel flapped his lanyard at one of the guards.

"Get that checked out," Ed said to the guard. "You'll probably find it's the one reported stolen earlier. That'll be enough to hold him with for now. We'll add to his tally later."

"What did he do with the dog?" Toby asked. "He didn't just abandon it."

"Ryan," said Pickle.

Of course! "Ryan!" Toby agreed. Before anybody could prevent him from doing so, he jumped onto the nearest grooming table and scanned the hall, properly studying the crowd but concentrating more on those moving towards the rear exits.

"There!" he shouted.

"What?" Clarissa asked.

"Not what. Who! Ryan! Lionel's brother!"

Ed turned to her. "What?"

Clarissa stood on tiptoes. "Toby's seen the other man involved."

"Show me!"

Once again, they began to race along the hall, leaving Lionel with the security guards. Toby took the lead, Pickle at his heels, Ed following behind and

Clarissa and the rats bringing up the rear. At first, they struggled to wend their way through the crowds but, as they left the show ring behind, the stalls and concessions became increasingly sparse and there were far fewer participants to dodge.

Now they had a clearer view of people and dogs coming and going. A flash of gold alerted Toby to a wagging tail. Hurrying after that first glint, he spotted the white fluffy bottom of a golden retriever walking happily on a lead alongside a man who may well have been his owner, except, when the man glanced fearfully over his shoulder, Toby could clearly make out a black eye and a split eyebrow.

Ryan!

"He's here! He's here! He's here!" Toby barked. "He's here!"

As Ed raced up to Ryan, Ryan folded like a deck of cards. He dropped the golden retriever's lead and held up his hands. The retriever bounced around the newcomers with glee. "Hey guys!" he sang. "How are you? Has anyone seen my mum? I've been having the most awesome adventure! Does anyone want to go for a run? Or a swim? Or shall we play fetch? Or ... or—"

"See what I mean? Totally exhausting,"

complained Pickle. "You really need to chill, man," she told the retriever.

"Is this the right dog?" Ed asked.

"Yes!" said Toby.

"It is," Clarissa confirmed.

"Keep your hands where I can see them," Ed instructed Ryan. "What's your name, fella?"

"Ryan Puckey," said Ryan.

"Any ID on you?" Ed asked.

Satisfied that they had their men, Toby turned away, glancing idly down the aisle towards the loading dock. The only person in sight at the furthest reaches of Hall 9 was an old woman with a twisted walking stick, hobbling along by herself. Short and dumpy, her shoulders hunched, she wore a pretty but old-fashioned dress of blue flowers with green leaves on a cream background, and a matching blue cardigan despite the warmth of the day. She reached the loading dock, opting to open one of the narrow doors to the side of the double gates. As she pulled it open, the sunshine spilled through, lighting her from behind. She turned partially, her gaze falling on Toby ...

He found it unsettling ... the steady knowingness of that gaze ... the glint of silver.

Toby shivered. It had to have been a trick of the light. Surely–

Then she smiled ...

And disappeared ...

And the door clanged as it closed.

But not behind her ...

Because it was as though she had never been there.

CHAPTER THIRTY

Toby stood stock still, staring at where the woman had been.

This woman hadn't resembled the one he'd seen in the country house. That woman had been taller—or at least less hunched—and younger. You might not have defined that woman as old at all, unless you weren't yet two years of age, like Toby.

But he knew better.

Perhaps they were mother and daughter, and only one of them was calling the shots.

"Your attention, please. Your attention, please," sang the tannoy. It had been making the occasional announcement since Toby had arrived at the NEC, but most of these had gone something along the lines of asking for judges to go to a specific ring or first aiders to a particular hall or someone to contact reception and so on. This was the first public announcement Toby had heard.

"We have an abandoned poodle ringside in Hall 9. Would the poodle's owner please make their way to the ring at the earliest opportunity to be reunited with her."

"Alright, Toby?" Clarissa appeared at his side and clipped her lead to his collar.

"I think I saw the old woman," Toby told her. "Their boss."

"The one you saw before?" Clarissa asked, peering back over her shoulder and wondering whether she should alert Ed.

"Not the same one—"

"Then how can we know it's her?" Clarissa asked. "Ed will only say we need more evidence."

"Perhaps Ryan and Lionel will come clean and drop her in it," Toby replied, somewhat wistfully. He had a feeling they wouldn't admit to murder, let alone dare to point the finger of blame at someone else.

"Perhaps. I think—"

"Your attention, please. Your attention, please," the tannoy piped up again. "We have an abandoned poodle ringside in Hall 9. Would the poodle's owner please make their way to the ring at the earliest opportunity to be reunited with her, or alternative arrangements for her safekeeping will be made."

Toby cocked his head. Okay. It was probably a coincidence, but hadn't the brothers been discussing the old woman showing dogs today? What if the poodle in question—

"Pickle!" Toby barked, and she scurried over. "There's an abandoned poodle over by the show ring."

Pickle's ears pricked up. "You don't think it could be Candy—?"

"I don't know, but let's go and take a look. You know Candy, and I don't." Toby began to trot towards the ring but didn't get very far because Clarissa was holding the lead.

"You're going to have to let go," he told her.

"I'll do nothing of the kind. We've caused enough trouble."

"Then you'll have to come with us." Toby tugged her. "We need to get to the ring, quickly, before they take her away."

"Take who away?" Clarissa asked, standing her ground.

"The poodle!"

Finally some light of understanding filtered into

Clarissa's brain and, after trying—and failing—to catch Ed's attention—he was still busy with Ryan and the security guards—she allowed herself to be led ringside.

At first there was a lot of confusion because the place was simply swarming with white poodles, but there, next to the registration table, a man in a suit and the obligatory lanyard and a woman wearing a t-shirt with the word *Fluffts* embroidered across it were standing together holding a lost-looking poodle on her lead and talking earnestly to each other.

Pickle paused. "Ha," she said. "Ha."

"Is that a good 'ha' or a bad 'ha'?" asked Toby.

Pickle's voice was soft, almost lost in the hubbub of the hall. "It's a good 'ha'. It's her. It's my sister. That's Candy!" She leapt forward, almost pulling Clarissa over. "Candy!" she cried. "Candy!"

Candy, almost a carbon copy of Pickle, cowered away for a moment then, realising who was mobbing her, lifted her snout and began to bray. The poodles danced and pranced together like a pair of stags, becoming so entangled that both the Fluffts official and Clarissa were forced to drop their leads.

The official laughed at the dogs' antics. "I should ask you whether this is your dog, madam, but judging by this reunion, I don't need to."

"Erm ..." Clarissa grimaced. "Actually, it's a little more complicated than that."

"Nothing we can't sort out, I'm sure," said the judge, smiling. "Here at Fluffts we always like to do the right things by our dogs."

"Do you?" Toby perked up at this. He smiled at the judge. "About that ... I'm famished! I don't suppose there's a sammich stall, is there?"

EPILOGUE

The final glance from the old woman in Hall 9 continued to bother Toby no end.

Even a couple of days later, when Ed came to visit Clarissa and fill in all the post-arrest details, he couldn't shake it off.

"You'll be delighted to hear that both Lionel and Ryan have been charged with murder," Ed told them as he sipped a beer in the garden. He was wearing a fleece because the night was cooler than of late. The leaves were beginning to turn, and there was the faintest scent of woodsmoke. Autumn wasn't far away.

Toby, relaxing on the threshold of his wizard shack, eyed Ed sceptically. "What about charges related to dognapping?" he wanted to know.

"Will you be able to make the dog theft charges stick?" Clarissa dutifully asked.

"Possibly." Ed shrugged. "It may be that we go with the one that's going to carry the longest sentence and the greatest chance of success. But in Ryan's case, it's likely he'll be charged with both. It's a little more circumstantial in Lionel's case, although we do have CCTV of him wheeling the caretaker's trolley around."

"That's something," said Toby, and lay his head down on the step, half his mind on Ed's conversation and half on his own preoccupations.

"We investigated the house you were telling me about," Ed was saying, referring to the country house where the Puckeys had been located. "It belongs to an Adalin Minovska, a Russian émigré or something, but there's no-one there. It's shut up. Almost completely derelict. It does look like a couple of dogs had been housed there though, and we did find some of the Puckeys' belongings."

And that's something, too, thought Toby.

He'd had a quiet couple of days now that Pickle and Candy had been reunited with Pea. He'd actually missed Pickle far more than he'd expected to. She'd been annoying at first, but once she'd done away with her whole arrogant I'm-a-princess persona, she'd turned out to be quite the feisty warrior.

Admirable, really. Credit where credit's due.

Then, once the poodles had been reunited with Pea—who couldn't bear to spend another moment without Pickle, apparently—there had been the small question of the rats. As he'd promised, Toby had had to escort Pom and Sal to West Hill. That had been comparatively easy because Clarissa had agreed to take them up there, and then she and Toby had stood by while Pom had enquired in several different drains and boltholes for family members.

Eventually, with a grateful wave and a swish of their tails, the pair had disappeared.

And that had been that.

But that's also something, Toby told himself. Better they went home than stayed here and were eaten by Moriarty or set upon by the Mayflower Lane Mafia for crimes against the brotherhood or some such.

"Toby doesn't seem to be his normal effervescent self," Ed remarked.

"A little bit lonely, I think," said Clarissa, wise in the ways of the hound she loved. "He'll be fine."

Will I though? thought Toby.

But that wasn't it. Not really. Partly, maybe.

Ever since that day at the country house, after that long, long walk home, his dreams had been full of strange shadows and women with glinting eyes. The more he thought about the mansion house hidden away on the road to Lyme Regis, the more convinced he became that the house had been enchanted somehow.

And the more he considered the woman with the silver eyes, the more he felt certain they'd met before.

That they were old foes.

"Erm ... excuse me?" A squeaking interrupted Toby's contemplation. He glanced to his right to see Sal standing a couple of yards away, a sardine can tucked under his arm. The rat cocked his head as Toby noticed him. "Howyadoin'?"

"Okay. I guess," said Toby, puzzled. "What are you doing back here?"

"Well, ain't that a story and a half? See, the thing is, I don't think Salvatore Messio is cut out to be part of the West Hill mob."

Toby stood to greet him. "Didn't they accept you?"

"Oh, it ain't that, it ain't that. Y'know ... Pom's family, they was happy for me to stay with them, but they're cut from a whole different cloth, right? I couldn't settle. That ain't where I belong."

"Are you going to go back to Mayflower Lane?" Toby asked with some alarm. Having met Persil Sollozzo and Cheeto Goryonli, he wasn't sure that doing so would be a wise move on Sal's behalf.

"Ya. Maybe. Maybe." Sal shrugged. "Maybe I'll try somewhere else. Ya never know. I might get lucky." He hitched the sardine can higher under his armpit. "Anyways, I thought I'd pop by and let ya know, y'know?"

"That's big," Toby said. "Good luck to you, brother."

"Yeah." Sal nodded enthusiastically. "You too, man, you too."

He ambled away, Toby watching him. Clarissa and Ed were still talking. They hadn't noticed Sal's arrival. They wouldn't notice him depart. How sad to be a creature that people actively avoid or ignore, that so many hoomans dislike.

He and Sal had had their differences, but he wasn't a bad guy.

"Hey," Toby called.

Sal turned around, whiskers twitching. "Hey, yourself."

"If you fancy sharing the contents of that can with me, I'll share my basket with you."

"The contents of this can?" Sal held it up, beaming. *Princes Sardines in Tomato Sauce.* "These would go awfully nicely with some of your special homemade delectables. Whaddayasay?"

"I'm inclined to agree," Toby replied, stepping aside so that Sal could enter the wizard shack. "Come on in."

Sal hurried back, his eyes shining.

Toby waved him through the door. "You know we'll have to discuss some house rules if you're going to stay here—"

"Whatever you say, man!"

"No unauthorised taking of my dog biscuits—"

"I understand. Your delectables are your business, me ole mucker."

"And I'll have to introduce you to Moriarty, the neighbour's cat."

"I'm sure she's a peach."

"I wouldn't go that far," said Toby, and levitated his Quality Street tin of dog biscuits down from the shelf, his tummy feeling fuzzy and happy because he had a friend come to stay.

Funny that he'd been thinking murky thoughts

about a certain Pointy Woman, and yet Sal had turned up to banish some of that darkness.

Friends and foes.

The latter would have to wait while Toby took care of the former.

But take care of it, he would.

COMING SOON

Fancy reading more of Toby's adventures?

Up, Pup and Away: Spellbound Hound Magic and Mystery Book 7

Toby's been building up quite a reputation for himself.

Well, he likes to think so.

It's therefore no surprise that when things go wrong for any of his canine friends, he gets called in to help them out. Lost puppies? No problem! Dognapping victim? Piece of cake.

COMING SOON

There's no mystery that our intrepid hound won't try to solve.

But this time it's personal.

The Pointy Woman is back ... and Toby has a rather large bone to pick with her.

Available for preorder on Amazon.

ALSO BY JEANNIE WYCHERLEY

Spellbound Hound

(*in reading order*)

Ain't Nothing but a Pound Dog: Spellbound Hound Magic and Mystery Book 1

A Curse, a Coven and a Canine: Spellbound Hound Magic and Mystery Book 2

Bark Side of the Moon: Spellbound Hound Magic and Mystery Book 3

Master of Puppies: Spellbound Hound Magic and Mystery Book 4

Dem Bones, Dem Bones: Spellbound Hound Magic and Mystery Book 5

Born to be Styled: Spellbound Hound Magic and Mystery Book 6

Up, Pup and Away: Spellbound Hound Magic and Mystery Book 7 (Release March 2024)

Another One Bites the Crust: Spellbound Hound Magic and Mystery Book 8 (Release 2024)

The Complete Wonky Inn Series

(in chronological reading order)

The Wonkiest Witch: Wonky Inn Book 1

The Ghosts of Wonky Inn: Wonky Inn Book 2

Weird Wedding at Wonky Inn: Wonky Inn Book 3

The Witch Who Killed Christmas: Wonky Inn Christmas Special

Fearful Fortunes and Terrible Tarot: Wonky Inn Book 4

The Mystery of the Marsh Malaise: Wonky Inn Book 5

The Mysterious Mr Wylie: Wonky Inn Book 6

The Great Witchy Cake Off: Wonky Inn Book 7

Vengeful Vampire at Wonky Inn: Wonky Inn Book 8

Witching in a Winter Wonkyland: A Wonky Inn Christmas Cozy Special

A Gaggle of Ghastly Grandmamas: Wonky Inn Book 9

Magic, Murder and a Movie Star: Wonky Inn Book 10

O' Witchy Town of Whittlecombe: A Wonky Inn Christmas Cozy Special

Judge, Jury and Jailhouse Rockcakes: Wonky Inn Book 11

A Midsummer Night's Wonky: Wonky Inn Book 12

Halloween Heebie-Geebies: Wonky Inn Book 13

Owl I want for Witchmas is Hoo: A Wonky Inn Christmas Cozy Mystery

Oh Mummy!: Wonky Inn Book 14

Pieces of Hate: Wonky Inn Book 15

The Faery of Witchmas Past: A Wonky Inn Christmas Cozy Special

Wonkytonk Witch: A Wonky Inn Mystery (Release 14th June 2024)

A Wonky Apprentice: Wonky Inn Book 17

A Barbarous Band of Blood Brothers: Wonky Inn Book 18 (Release 29th April 2024)

The Witchy Wood and the Weirdly Wyse: Wonky Inn Book 19 (Release TBC 2024)

Wonderland Detective Agency

Dead as a Dodo: Wonderland Detective Agency Book 1

The Rabbit Hole Murders: Wonderland Detective Agency Book 2

Tweedledumb and Tweedledie: Wonderland Detective Agency Book 3

The Curious Incident at the Pig and Pepper: Wonderland Detective Agency Book 4

A Tragic Tea Party: Wonderland Detective Agency Book 5

The Pool of Tears: Wonderland Detective Agency Book 6

Into the Labyrinth: Wonderland Detective Agency Book 7 (Release TBC 2024)

The Municipality of Lost Souls

Midnight Garden: The Extra Ordinary World Novella Series Book 1

Beyond the Veil

Crone

A Concerto for the Dead and Dying

Deadly Encounters: A collection of short stories

Keepers of the Flame: A love story

With Peter Alderson Sharp

The Creature from the Grim Mire: A humorous Sci-fi, Time Travel and Alien Contact Mystery

Non-Fiction

Losing my best Friend: Thoughtful support for those affected by dog bereavement or pet loss

---

Follow Jeannie Wycherley

Buy me a coffee

www.buymeacoffee.com/jeanniewych

Find out more at on the website www.jeanniewycherley.co.uk

Or visit her on Facebook for her fiction

www.facebook.com/jeanniewycherley

Follow Jeannie on Instagram (for bears and books)

www.instagram.com/jeanniewycherley

See Jeannie on Tiktok @jeanniewycherley

Sign up for Jeannie's newsletter on her website

www.subscribepage.com/JeannieWycherleyWonky

Printed in Great Britain
by Amazon

60886571R00204